NEVER LAUGH AT LOVE

Anthea Forthingdale had made the most costly mistake of her life.

Granted she needed money to ease her mother and three sisters out of their impoverished existence. And granted Anthea's clever caricatures of London high society had been a smashing success: even the Prince Regent chuckled at her witty, anonymous parodies and a newspaper had offered her ten pounds outright for each drawing.

But to have submitted a caricature of her own alluring young Godmother with her illicit lover, the Duke of Axminster, for publication . . . Really, what had Anthea been thinking of? And now her Godmother's outraged husband was threatening his unfaithful wife with a messy divorce.

There was only one way out of this tempest Anthea had created with her silly scribblings. As the Duke proposed the solution, the poor young girl went cold with dread . . .

**A Regency Romance
by
BARBARA CARTLAND**

Bantam Books by Barbara Cartland
Ask your bookseller for the books you have missed

Barbara Cartland
Never Laugh at Love

NEVER LAUGH AT LOVE
A Bantam Book / October 1976

ISBN 0–553–02993–2

Published simultaneously in the United States and Canada.

Bantam Books are published by Bantam Books, Inc. Its trade-
mark, consisting of the words "Bantam Books" and the por-
trayal of a bantam, is registered in the United States Patent
Office and in other countries. Marca Registrada. Bantam
Books, Inc., 666 Fifth Avenue, New York, New York 10019.

PRINTED IN THE UNITED STATES OF AMERICA

Author's Note

James Gillray was the first master draughtsman to make caricature a primary occupation and he became the most ferocious and brilliant caricaturist of his time.

He was so popular that there were queues outside Humphrey's Print Shop, over which he lived, waiting for his latest cartoon. By the end of 1811, when he was still in his middle fifties, he was already half crazy, the victim of hard drinking from the terrific pressure of work.

Thomas Rowlandson came from the comfortable middle class and had art training in Paris and at the School of the Royal Academy.

He began as a painter of serious subjects. However, he lost so much money gambling that he turned to satirical cartoons.

George Cruikshank's work lacked Gillray's tremendous force and Rowlandson's zest. He was successful in his early twenties and lived, after fifty years of aggressive teetotalism, until 1878.

Chapter One

1817

"It has come! It has come!"

Chloe tore into the School-Room, where her sisters were sitting at the big table in the centre of the room.

"It has come!" she repeated.

"The letter?" Thais questioned.

"What else?" Chloe answered. "I was certain when I saw the Post Chaise turn in at the gate that something exciting was going to happen!"

"How do you know it is a letter from God-mama?" Anthea asked.

She spoke in a quieter tone, but there was no mistaking the excitement in her eyes.

In answer Chloe held up the letter, which the girls could all see was written on the most expensive white vellum paper, and addressed in flowery, elegant hand-writing to their mother.

"She has answered quickly," Thais said. "We did not expect to hear from her until at least the end of the week."

"I am sure she has said yes," Chloe remarked. "Oh, Anthea, think how exciting it will be!"

"Shall I go and tell Mama?" Phebe enquired.

She was the youngest of the sisters and was only ten. Chloe was sixteen and Thais a year older.

Phebe had fair hair and blue eyes and was in fact a small replica of Thais and they both looked exactly like their mother.

"No, you cannot disturb Mama," Anthea said quickly.

"Why not?" Chloe enquired.

1

"Because she is communicating with the Muse."

"Oh, Lord, not again!" Chloe exclaimed. "I suppose we dare not disturb her."

She looked enquiringly at Anthea as she spoke, as if she hoped her oldest sister would contradict her. But Anthea said firmly:

"No, of course not. You know how it upsets Mama when she is writing to have us interrupt her train of thought."

Chloe put the letter on the mantelshelf, propped up against the clock.

She gave a little sigh and said:

"I think I shall die of curiosity if Mama does not open it soon."

"It is only eleven o'clock," Anthea said. "We shall just have to wait until it is time for luncheon."

Thais groaned.

"Why ever did she have to have a visitation today of all days?"

"I think she has been thinking over a poem for some time," Anthea answered. "I know what it means when she gets that far-away look in her eyes."

"If only they were good enough, we might sell them," Chloe said.

"Of course we could not do that," Anthea retorted.

"Why not?" Chloe enquired. "They say that Lord Byron has made an absolute fortune out of his poems. I am sure Mama's are nearly as good."

"I am certain she would be extremely shocked at the idea of commercialising her art," Anthea said. "So you are not to suggest it to her, Chloe—it would only worry her."

"It is far more worrying to be without money," Thais interposed in a practical tone. "Supposing your God-mama will have you stay with her in London, Anthea, what do you think you are going to wear?"

"I made myself a new gown last week," Anthea replied.

"That is not going to take you very far," Thais said. "Not if one is to believe the *Ladies' Journal!* They say a débutante requires at least ten gowns for a Season in London."

"If I do go, which I very much doubt," Anthea said, "then there is only a month of the Season left. We all know that the Prince Regent goes to Brighton at the beginning of June."

"Well, even for a month you will need more than one gown," Thais retorted.

At seventeen Thais was very clothes-conscious.

Of the four sisters, she most resented having only the cheapest materials with which to make their own gowns and being unable to afford none of the ornamentation which the *Ladies' Journal* said was essential if one was to be stylish.

It was true, Anthea thought, that her appearance would be lamentable if she did go to London and, as hr mother confidently expected, moved in the smart Society in which her God-mother, the Countess of Sheldon, was a leading light.

Actually, Anthea had never thought for a moment that her mother's sudden idea of sending her to London for the Season would prove to be anything but a pipe-dream.

Always vague, always, as her husband had said so often, with her head in the clouds, Lady Forthingdale had failed to realise that at nineteen Anthea, her oldest daughter, might expect a more amusing existence than could be provided in the small house where they lived in an obscure Yorkshire village.

It had been, of all unexpected people, the local Vicar who had awakened her to her responsibilities.

He had been obliging enough after Sir Walcott Forthingdale's death to give the younger girls, Thais, Chloe and Phebe, lessons in history, Scripture, and Latin.

They learnt French from a Frenchwoman who, having previously taught her native language at a young ladies' Seminary in Harrogate, had retired to the village when the school had no further use for her.

Lady Forthingdale paid extremely little for the lessons, but Anthea always thought that Mademoiselle

enjoyed them far more than her pupils, simply because
she felt lonely in her cottage and longed for someone
to talk to.

The Vicar, calling on Lady Forthingdale to report
on Phebe's progress in Latin, had remarked on leaving:

"I often think, My Lady, how fortunate you are
to have such charming and delightful daughters. It will
undoubtedly be a sad day when they marry and leave
home, which of course Miss Anthea might do at any
time."

"Marry?—Anthea?" Lady Forthingdale had exclaimed.

"I believe she has passed her nineteenth birthday," the Vicar replied. "A time when most young
ladies, especially one as pretty as Miss Anthea, begin
to think of setting up a home of their own."

"Yes, of course, Vicar," Lady Forthingdale had
agreed.

But when he had gone she had sent for Anthea
and said in a self-reproachful manner:

"Dearest, how could I have been so thoughtless? I
had forgotten that you were nineteen! It is remiss of
me to have done nothing about it."

"About what, Mama?" Anthea answered.

"About making your début," Lady Forthingdale
replied.

"Me, Mama? But how could it be possible?"

"It was what your father and I always intended,"
Lady Forthingdale said. "But I have been so distressed, so helpless, since he was killed that it never
struck me how old you were."

"Very old, Mama!" Anthea laughed. "Soon my
teeth will be falling out and my hair going grey!"

"I am talking seriously, Anthea," Lady Forthingdale said reprovingly. "We may be poor, but the Forthingdales have been respected in Yorkshire for hundreds of years, and my own family came to England
with William the Conqueror."

"Yes, I know, Mama," Anthea said, "but being
blue-blooded does not pay the bills, and it certainly
will not provide for a Season in London."

Since her father's death she had taken over the running of the house and the paying of the bills.

Better than anyone else, she realised how little they all had to live on, and how careful they had to be with every penny.

"I was not suggesting that we should pay for you in London," Lady Forthingdale said. "I am not quite as stupid as that, Anthea."

"Who else is likely to do so? You know how few relations we have."

"I would not ask your father's relations to help, not even if we were starving in the gutter!" Lady Forthingdale said with a sudden note of anger in her soft, musical voice. "They were always horrible to me because they expected your father to marry money. In fact they never forgave him."

"He fell in love with you, Mama," Anthea said, "and that is not surprising. You have always been the most beautiful person I have ever seen in my life."

Lady Forthingdale smiled.

"You take after your Papa, dearest, and while he was exceedingly handsome, you are very pretty."

That was certainly true, but while Anthea had her father's dark hair, she had very large green-grey eyes which sparkled mischievously and a curving, smiling mouth that was complemented by two dimples in either of her cheeks.

Ever since she had been a baby in a cradle, anyone who looked at Anthea had smiled at her, and she had a laugh which made people laugh with her.

"You are flattering me, Mama!" she said now. "But do go on! I adore being paid compliments!"

"Which should not be given by your mother," Lady Forthingdale said sharply. "Oh, how could I have been so selfish and forgetful as not to have thought of this before?"

"Thought of what?" Anthea asked.

"Of writing to your God-mother, my friend Delphine, the Countess of Sheldon."

Galvanised by her remorse at being so negligent, Lady Forthingdale had sat down there and then and written to the Countess of Sheldon to ask if in memory of their old friendship she would do her a great favour and invite Anthea to stay with her in London.

> She has been such a Wonderful Daughter to me since my Beloved Husband's Death, that in my Grief and Distress I completely overlooked the fact that this Year, now that we are out of mourning, Anthea should have appeared in Society.
>
> I have always remembered Your own Ball and how Beautiful You looked, Delphine, and how every man was at Your Feet. I am therefore begging You to remember Anthea, your God-daughter, and let Her just for a few weeks, sample the Delights of London and meet a few Young Men, who, you will understand, are sadly lacking in this small Village.

She went on to recall how delighted Delphine had been when at the age of fifteen and just after her confirmation Lady Forthingdale had asked her to be Godmother to her first child.

Delphine's parents had lived in Essex, a mile from Lady Forthingdale's. Their mothers were close friends and their fathers were joint-Masters of the local foxhounds.

At fifteen, Delphine had adored with an adolescent passion the beautiful Christobel, who, three years her senior, had married the dashing Sir Walcott Forthingdale almost as soon as she left the School-Room.

Sophisticated, worldly, and inclined to be somewhat of a Rake, Sir Walcott had been bowled over by Christobel the moment he saw her at her first Ball.

From that time he had never left her side, and disregarding all protests from her parents they had been married at the end of the year.

Anthea had been born when her mother was just nineteen and had gone back to her parents' house for her confinement.

Delphine had been a daily visitor, and when the

baby was born she appeared to adore Anthea as much as she adored her mother.

It had been therefore an inexpressible thrill when Lady Forthingdale had suggested that Delphine should be one of the God-mothers at Anthea's Christening.

But after that they had seen very little of each other.

Sir Walcott had settled down on his family Estates in Yorkshire and he was not really to blame for the fact that the rents he raised could not pay for the upkeep.

Gradually with the passing years and the financial difficulties which arose during the war with Napoleon, their income shrunk so that when he was killed at Waterloo there was in fact very little left.

"You are too old! How can you possibly leave me?" Lady Forthingdale had protested when Sir Walcott insisted on rejoining his Regiment and buying himself a Captaincy.

"I am damned if I am going to sit here rotting," he had replied, "and let all my friends fight for me."

He had however listened to her pleas until after the battle of Trafalgar, when everyone had been quite certain that the war would be over very quickly.

"I have to be in at the kill!" he had said. "I have shirked my fences long enough."

He had gone off to fight under Wellington, but fortunately for Lady Forthingdale's peace of mind, he was not posted to the Peninsula.

But when finally the Army had proceeded to Brussels for the final showdown with Napoleon, Sir Walcott was with the Cavalry.

It had been inevitable, Anthea had thought when they heard of his death, that he should be amongst those who made the wild Cavalry charge at the beginning of the battle in which there were twenty-five hundred casualties.

"It is just the way Papa would have wished to die," she had told her broken-hearted mother, realising it was no consolation to those left behind.

But she knew that her father, who had always

been a thruster in the hunting-field, would never have held back or been content not to be first in the field of battle.

They had been forced to leave the house in which they had lived all their lives, and because the Estate was in bad repair the small amount they received for it had mostly gone in paying Sir Walcott's debts.

There had been, however, enough to buy the small house in Smaller Shireoaks, in which they now lived, and to invest the surplus to bring in a minute income every year on which they all had to live.

It had never even crossed Anthea's mind that she should be doing anything else but looking after her mother and sisters.

Occasionally there was a Ball in the neighbourhood to which she was invited and in fact she had attended two last winter after they were out of mourning.

But while she had plenty of partners they were mostly married men or youths whose mothers kept a strict eye on them and had no intention of allowing them to become involved with "that penniless Forthingdale girl, however pretty she might be!"

When the letter had actually been sent to the Countess of Sheldon, Anthea had allowed herself a few day-dreams in which she took London by storm and found herself not only a suitable husband, but also one rich enough to help her sisters.

Now that the idea had been put into her head, she realised that it was essential for Thais, who was so pretty, to "come out" the following year.

"Even then she will be older than most of the other débutantes," Anthea reasoned, "and after her there will be Chloe and lastly Phebe. I must find myself a husband who will allow me to entertain for each one of them in turn!"

At the same time, she was well aware that her mother had not seen the Countess of Sheldon for more than eight years.

People altered, drifted apart from their old friends, and, as Anthea was well aware, did not wish to be encumbered with other people's daughters.

She calculated without much difficulty that the

Countess was now thirty-four, and although she knew little of Social life she could not help feeling that it was rather young to undertake the duties of a Chaperon.

However, the letter had gone to London, and while Anthea could not believe that the Countess would totally ignore her mother's appeal, she was quite certain it was a ninety-nine-to-one chance that she would say "No."

"I cannot wait an hour and a half for Mama to open that letter," Thais said, sitting down at the School-Room table. "Shall we steam it open and see what is inside?"

"Oh, yes, let us do that!" Chloe cried.

"Certainly not!" Anthea said automatically. "You know that would be most underhand and ill-bred, and certainly unbecoming to a Lady of Fashion!"

"From all I read of Ladies of Fashion," Thais said, "they do all sorts of things that would be considered unladylike. In the novel I have just finished, the heroine was always listening at key-holes."

"Servants do that—not heroines," Anthea said. "I cannot think where you find such books. Certainly not in Papa's Library . . . or the Vicar's."

Thais giggled and looked exceedingly pretty as she did so.

"I borrowed it from Ellen."

"Ellen?"

Thais did not answer and Anthea said:

"Do you mean Ellen at the Dog and Duck?"

"She has a gentleman-friend who brings them to her regularly," Thais admitted.

"Oh, Thais, how can you?" Anthea protested. "I am sure Mama would have a fit if she thought you were friendly with Ellen, even though she is a very kind woman."

At the same time, it came home to her very forcibly that Thais ought to have more-suitable friends than the bar-maid at the Dog and Duck.

She was only just seventeen the previous month, but she had already lost what her father used to call "puppyfat" and was so pretty that even the choir-boys stared at her when she was in Church.

'It is Thais who should go to London, not me,' Anthea thought, and wondered whether her God-mother, if she sent an invitation, would accept Thais as a substitute for herself.

"What can Mama be writing now?" Chloe asked.

"I think she is going through a religious phase," Thais answered.

"We are lucky that it did not happen before we were born. Otherwise I am certain one of us would have been christened Jezebel or Magdalene!" Chloe said.

They all laughed.

'To Chloe's heart young Cupid shyly stole,' Anthea murmured beneath her breath.

But she did not say it aloud; they had teased Chloe too often with the verse.

"It could not be worse than being called Chloe," her sister went on despairingly. "Why, oh why did Mama have a William Blake period when I was born?"

"I do not think mine is much better," Thais said. "No-one can ever pronounce my name properly."

"Think how romantic it is," Phebe said.

She sprang to her feet to recite dramatically:

> *The lovely Thais at his side*
> *Sat like a blooming Eastern bride*
> *In flow'r of youth and beauty's pride.*

"Oh, shut up!" Thais cried, and picking up one of the books that lay on the table threw it at her.

The girls, with the exception of Anthea, all hated their names.

She would read Robert Herrick's ode: "To Anthea! Ah, my Anthea!" and wonder if it would ever come true in her life.

> *Give me a kiss and to that kiss a score;*
> *Then to that twenty add a hundred more.*

Would a man ever say that to her? And what would she feel if he did?

"I cannot think why Mama could not have chosen a name from 'The Vicar of Wakefield,' " Chloe was saying. "When she was reading it to us, I thought that if I did anything wrong I could always quote her source by saying:

> *When a lovely woman stoops to folly*
> *And finds too late that men betray . . .*

"It might be something to remember as a precaution rather than an excuse," Anthea remarked.

"I wonder what sort of folly the poet was thinking about," Phebe asked.

No-one answered her and she said defiantly:

"If Papa were alive, I should ask him."

"Well, he is not!" Anthea said. "And you are not to bother Mama."

It was a rule in the house that their mother was never to be bothered.

They all loved the sweet, rather ineffective person she had become since her husband had been killed.

It was a point of honour to protect her from all the difficulties that she made little effort to understand, but which gave her sleepless nights when she knew about them.

Anthea often thought that her mother wrote poetry whenever she wished to escape from anything unpleasant.

It was certainly what she had done during her husband's lifetime, and now she seemed to become more and more immersed in writing long poems, which she read to her daughters and then forgot.

For the first time Anthea wondered if in fact it would be possible to sell what her mother had written.

Then she told herself that while the idea would doubtless horrify the author, it was very unlikely that any publisher would be interested.

From all they had read in the magazines, Lord Byron's works had been an overwhelming success.

But the scandals that surrounded him compelled him to go abroad the previous year, and Anthea suspected that when he was no longer present to be talked about and be the centre of attraction, the sales might drop.

Who, she asked herself with practical common sense, would be concerned with poems written by a lady in the wilds of Yorkshire, who would certainly not be a talking-point for the gay, frivolous Socialites who enjoyed Lord Byron's effusions?

"You know it is rather sad," she said aloud, "that none of us have any salable talents."

"I am writing a novel," Thais said.

"Yes, I know," Anthea answered. "But you have been writing it for the last three years and as far as I can make out you have only got to chapter five. By the time you have finished in another twenty years it will not matter whether with the sales you can buy a pretty gown or an ugly one."

She bent her back and with shaking hands, faltered in a quavering voice:

"All my own . . . work, help . . . a poor old woman . . . pretty lady . . . who has given the best years of . . . her life . . ."

There was a burst of laughter.

Anthea's impersonations were always life-like and her sisters now recognised old Mrs. Ridgewell, who was the village beggar.

"It is very difficult to write a novel," Thais said with dignity, "and besides it takes me so long because I cannot spell!"

"I suppose I might sell some of my water-colour sketches," Anthea remarked reflectively.

Chloe laughed.

"The last time you put one in the village Bazaar it stuck and stuck. It was only when I reduced it to three pence that it was sold, and then it was only because Mrs. Briggs liked the frame!"

Anthea sighed.

"I noticed when I went to see her last week because she was ill that she had taken out my picture and the frame had a pressed rose in it which one of her grandchildren had sent to her!"

"Well, it certainly does not look as if we shall make any money that way," Chloe said. "I have often thought that I might give riding-lessons for anyone who would pay me."

"And who is likely to do that?" Thais enquired. "Anyone in the village who has an animal with four legs rides it anyway and the County when they go hunting certainly do not wish to be taught by you."

Chloe sighed.

"I would give anything for a good horse! It is absolutely sickening that now that Papa is dead we have only old Dobbin to take Mama out when she wants to go anywhere, which is very seldom."

"We cannot afford anything better," Anthea said, "and Dobbin must be getting on for twelve years old. You are not to ride him hard, Chloe. If he falls dead, we should never be able to buy another one."

"Money! Money! Money!" Chloe declared. "No-one talks of anything else in this house."

"It all comes back to what I asked originally," Thais said. "What is Anthea going to wear if she goes to London?"

"I am going to wear the clothes I already have with the new ones which you will all have to make for me."

Her sisters stared at her wide-eyed and she went on:

"I have thought about this just in case God-mama says she will have me. I am quite certain that we are clever enough to copy the designs in the latest *Ladies' Journal*, so that I shall be presentable, if not spectacular!"

"You will look like a country mouse," Chloe said frankly.

"Very well . . . a country mouse," Anthea agreed. "But if the opportunity arises I am not going to refuse to go to London, because if I get there I have a feeling it would be to the advantage of all of us."

There was a moment's silence, then Thais said:

"You mean . . . you would find a husband?"

"If I . . . can."

"I do not want you to get married," Phebe said,
her voice rising to a wail. "If you get married, Anthea,
you will go away and leave us. It would be horrid without you—it would really!"

She got up from the table as she spoke and rushed
round to the other side to put her arms round Anthea's
neck.

"We love you, Anthea! We cannot let you go away
and marry some horrid man who will never be as fond
of you as we are."

"Perhaps I will marry a nice man who will have
you all to stay," Anthea said, "who would lend Chloe
his horses to ride and give a Ball for Thais."

"Do you really think you could do that?" Thais
asked.

"I can at least try," Anthea answered.

As she looked at her sisters' serious faces and wide
eyes, the dimples showed in her cheeks and she said:

"If I go to London I shall wear a placard round
my neck saying: *Three sisters to support! Please help
with a wedding-ring!*"

The girls all dissolved into laughter and at that
moment the door opened and Lady Forthingdale came
in.

She moved slowly and there was a far-away look
in her eyes that they all knew meant that she was in
the midst of being inspired by the Muse.

"I need your help, girls," she said. "I cannot get
any further with my poem."

It said a great deal for the respect in which her
daughters held Lady Forthingdale's talent that none of
them for the moment mentioned the letter on the mantelshelf.

Instead they were silent as their mother, completely
unselfconscious, stood just inside the door and lifting
one white hand with its long, thin fingers recited:

> *In dying are we born,*
> *And if some part in this pale earth*
> *Must fade because I hold you in my arms,*
> *Why then I would embrace the cross itself*

If through the sacrifice of self be found
The glory of a love which must be God's."

"That is lovely, Mama!" Anthea exclaimed as she finished.

"One of your best!" Thais agreed.

"But what comes next?" Lady Forthingdale asked. "That is what I cannot determine."

"You will have inspiration later on," Anthea said. "It is nearly luncheon-time, Mama. I was just going to come and interrupt you anyway."

"This morning the first part of the poem seemed to flow quite smoothly," Lady Forthingdale went on, but Anthea could bear it no longer.

"There is a letter, Mama! It arrived over an hour ago!"

The words seemed to burst from her and Lady Forthingdale looked at her daughter in astonishment before she said in quite genuine bewilderment:

"Letter? What letter?"

"A letter from London, Mama."

"From London? Oh—from Delphine Sheldon. I had forgotten. Do you mean there is an answer to mine?"

"Yes, Mama."

Chloe jumped up to take the letter from the mantelshelf and put it in her mother's hand.

"It must have come very quickly," Lady Forthingdale said in surprise.

"It flew here on the wings of a dove!" Chloe said irrepressibly. "Open it, Mama! Open it and see what she says!"

Very slowly, as it seemed to her daughters watching her, Lady Forthingdale opened the letter.

She began to read it. Then Chloe could not bear the tension.

"Read it aloud, Mama! Please read it aloud!"

"Yes, of course," Lady Forthingdale agreed. "I was forgetting how interested you would all be, especially Anthea."

She smiled at her oldest daughter before she held up the letter and read it aloud.

Sheldon House,
Curzon Street,
London

Dearest Christobel:

It was a Surprise and such a very Pleasant One to hear from You after all these Years. I have often thought about You and I was indeed most deeply Distressed to hear that Sir Walcott had been killed at Waterloo. So many of our Splendid and Brave men died there to save the world from that Monster Napoleon Bonaparte.

Of course I shall be Delighted to have my God-daughter, Anthea, to stay with Me here in London. It is a great Pity that We did not think of it Sooner as, Alas, there is not very much Left of the Season in which to present Her to the Fashionable World.

I feel however I can give Her a very Enjoyable time and suggest She leaves Immediately.

It will not be possible for Me to send His Lordship's horses as far as Yorkshire, but if You can convey Her to the White Horse at Eaton Socom this Friday I will Arrange for an Abigail to look after Her that Night, and for our Travelling-Carriage to convey them both to London the following Morning.

I send You my Affectionate Greetings, Dearest Christobel, and will look forward to seeing My God-daughter, whom I remember as a very attractive Child. She will bring with Her Memories of the happy times We spent together so many Years ago. Oh, Dear, how quickly Time passes!

Yours lovingly, and with unchanging Affection,

Delphine Sheldon

Lady Forthingdale finished reading the letter and Chloe gave a hoot of joy and excitement.

"She has accepted! She has accepted! Oh, Anthea, do you hear? You are to go to London!"

Chloe glanced round the room with excitement, but Anthea, who had risen to her feet, stood looking at her mother with worried eyes.

"Friday evening," she said. "Do you realise, Mama, that that means I have only tomorrow to get ready for the visit?"

"That will give you plenty of time to pack," Lady Forthingdale replied vaguely.

"But, Mama . . ." Anthea began.

As she spoke she caught Thais's eye and realised there was no point in saying any more.

Her mother would only be distressed if she said that she had nothing to wear.

After all, she thought, even a week would not be enough to replenish or create a wardrobe in the style which would be expected in London.

"I shall just have to explain to my God-mother," she told herself, "that she must put up with me as I am!"

"I think it is very kind of Delphine," Lady Forthingdale was saying gently. "But I was quite certain she would not fail me. As I have always said to you all, it is friendship that counts in life and really friends never alter."

* * *

In London the Countess of Sheldon was entertaining the Duke of Axminster in her elegant Salon.

He had just returned from Newmarket where he had been in attendance on the Prince Regent, and finding a note from Her Ladyship awaiting him at Axminster House, he had answered the summons immediately without changing his driving-clothes.

His close-fitting breeches and polished Hessian boots made him, with his grey whipcord jacket, look even more handsome and elegant than usual.

There was an expression on his face as he regarded the Countess which softened the usual, rather hard arrogance of his eyes.

"I came as soon as I got back" he said. "Your note sounded urgent."

"It was," Delphine Sheldon said briefly. "We have had, Garth, the most fantastic piece of good fortune!"

"What is that?" the Duke enquired.

"I am so glad you were away the last week or you would have been as desperate as I was."

"What happened?"

"Edward suddenly decided that he would return to the country. You know how he hates London, and something had upset him at the Club! I do not know what it was, but he came back in a towering rage and said we were to leave on Tuesday and he was closing the house."

"Good God!" the Duke ejaculated. "What did you do?"

"I argued with him, I pleaded, but he was adamant! You know how he loves being at Sheldon. He was just determined to get back there."

The Countess paused, then she said:

"I loathe the country, and that ghastly mother-in-law of mine makes it a hell on earth. Besides, I should die if I could not see you!"

"You know what it would mean to me also."

"Yes, of course, but I could hardly tell Edward that!"

"You said we have had a stroke of good fortune," the Duke prompted.

"I was just going to tell you about it but I can assure you, Garth, it was a very near thing that I was not swept away from you and incarcerated in that mausoleum in the backwoods of Wiltshire!"

"Well, you are still here and that is all that concerns me at the moment," the Duke said with a smile.

"And it concerns me," Delphine Sheldon said softly.

She put out her hand to him as she spoke and he kissed her fingers.

She wondered if there was any other man in London who could do it so gracefully, while looking so disturbingly masculine.

"You look very lovely!" he said. "But go on with your story."

"I was in despair," the Countess said. "When Edward makes up his mind nothing will alter it. It is like banging one's head against the Rock of Gibraltar!"

"But you succeeded in changing his decision!" the Duke again prompted.

He found it slightly irritating that the Countess always took a long time in coming to the point of a story.

"That was when a miracle happened," she said. "Out of the blue, at the very last moment, when I had given up hope and my maid was actually packing my trunks, there arrived a letter from Lady Forthingdale!"

The Duke looked puzzled.

"Do I know her?"

"No, of course not. She lives in Yorkshire and we were friends when I was a girl."

The Duke waited.

"I had not heard from her for eight years, but now she has written to me," the Countess said, "asking if she could send her daughter, who is my God-child, to London for what remains of the Season."

She paused expectantly, but for a moment the Duke was unresponsive.

"Do you not understand?" she asked at length. "Oh, Garth, do not be so obtuse. When I showed the letter to Edward he quite saw that I had a duty to my God-daughter, and I could not very well refuse her mother's request."

"Do you mean that you are going to have the girl here?"

"Of course I am going to have the girl here," the Countess replied. "I would have Medusa here, or whatever that monster was called who had the snakes in her hair, if it meant I could stay in London!"

She gave a little sigh of sheer happiness.

"Do you not understand?" she asked. "It means that Edward has gone to Sheldon and I can remain here until the end of the Season!"

"He will really allow you to stay here alone?"

"Not alone," the Countess corrected, "but with my

God-daughter, chaperoning her in the most respectable manner to all the most important parties, and to Almack's. In fact I shall be a Dowager, Garth, sitting on the dais and behaving with the utmost propriety."

"Not as far as I am concerned, I hope!" the Duke objected.

The Countess laughed.

"No, of course not! But that is what Edward believes, and you know what a stickler he is for doing the right thing. Especially when it concerns one's duty! That is what I persuaded him I owed to . . ."

She paused.

"What is the girl's name? I ought to remember. I was at her Christening. An . . . Anthea! Yes, of course. Anthea!"

She laughed.

"Anthea Forthingdale! Poor girl. What a mouthful!"

"It is, as you say, a piece of good fortune. I could not have borne your being taken away from me to Sheldon. It would have been very hard for me to find an excuse to drop in there."

"There will be no need for you to have any excuses to come here," the Countess said. "And not only has Edward gone, but he has also taken that doddering old Butler with him who I am convinced was always spying on me, and of course his personal valet and the groom who has been with the Sheldons for forty years —which is far too long for any servant to stay with anyone!"

She threw out her hands in an expressive gesture.

"So I have new staff and an open door and an open heart, my dearest, irresistibly handsome Garth!"

The Duke did what was expected of him and took the Countess in his arms.

*   *   *

It was an hour later that the Countess, looking at herself in her mirror as she dressed for dinner, thought how satisfactory life could be when one managed to get one's own way.

She had not exaggerated when she told the Duke

that she really was in despair at being taken to the country at a moment's notice, just because her husband was bored with London.

If Lady Forthingdale's letter had not arrived to save her, she would have had to do as her husband wanted.

She had been married when she was only eighteen, in the same hasty manner as her friend Christobel, but in her case it was a very different marriage.

The Earl of Sheldon, immensely rich and of considerable Social importance, had been a widower for ten years when he saw his future wife in the crowded Ball-Room at Devonshire House.

She had been among a number of débutantes who were present at one of the lavish and exclusive Balls which were given by the Duke and Duchess of Devonshire and attended by everyone who was of any importance in the *Beau Monde*.

Delphine had not been particularly outstanding amongst the other girls of her age. It may have been her red hair which attracted the Earl, or perhaps it was her youth which to a man satiated with sophistication had a charm of its own.

Yet the explanation may simply have been that love is unpredictable and no-one can be quite certain where Cupid's arrow is likely to strike next.

Whatever the reason, the Earl, who since he had been widowed had devoted himself to much older and more experienced beauties, had danced for the first time in many years with a débutante and lost his heart.

Delphine had been both intrigued and overwhelmed by his importance.

But even if she had wished to refuse such a matrimonial catch, it would have been impossible for her to do so.

Her father and mother were not unnaturally delighted at their daughter's success, and she was whisked up the aisle almost before she knew what was happening to her.

There was no doubt that at first she had been extremely happy.

The luxury with which her husband enveloped
her and the sophisticated Social World into which he
introduced her had an allure which kept her an adoring and faithful wife for at least ten years.

During this time she presented the Earl with two
sons and a daughter, and then began to think about
herself.

The Earl was getting older and he found the
country far more satisfying than London.

What was more, he had little in common with the
Regent.

In fact, he resented the manner in which the Heir
to the Throne, growing more and more frustrated at not
being King, expected fulsome adulation, uncritical
flattery, and undivided attention from all who surrounded him.

The Earl was too much of an individualist and too
egotistical himself to find Carlton House anything but
a bore.

While too experienced socially to show his boredom, he found it so much easier to live in the country,
where no demands were made upon him.

Delphine, on the contrary, found in London all
she desired in the way of amusement and interest.

This narrowed down eventually to any gentleman
who was prepared to succumb to her charms and cast
his heart at her feet.

The years had brought her a wholehearted appre-
ciation of her particular attractions and she had no desire to hide them under a bushel.

She was beautiful, she was *chic,* and the Earl's
importance made it easy for her to become a leader of
the gay, raffish, and extravagant Society which revolved
round Carlton House.

After she took her first lover, she had felt guilty.

But by the time their numbers had multiplied considerably, she was concerned only with keeping her
husband in ignorance of what was now vital to her
happiness.

She was in fact rather in awe of the Earl.

Although she could beguile and entice him into
doing most of the things she wished, there was a hard

core of obstinate determination on which she could make no impression.

This was obvious when it came to a choice between London and Sheldon, and on anything which concerned the honour of the family.

No amount of entreaty, pleading, or defiance would move the Earl on these matters, and Delphine knew it.

It was therefore, as she had said, a miracle that she had been reprieved at the eleventh hour from having to leave London and—more important—the Duke.

She had, as it happened, achieved the zenith of a long-treasured ambition when she succeeded in attracting the Duke of Axminster.

He had a reputation for being not only difficult, but also extremely fastidious.

He was of course pursued by every match-making mother in the length and breadth of England.

He was also sought after, chased, and hunted relentlessly by the Ladies of Fashion who counted their successes as a Red Indian counted the scalps on his belt.

It had taken time, a great deal of manoeuvring, and a lot of luck before the Duke became aware of Delphine's enticements, but finally she had "hooked him."

It was a triumph which was all the sweeter because she was in fact genuinely enamoured of the most eligible bachelor of the "Town" and veteran of an inordinate number of amatory campaigns.

It was not only his great possessions or even his undeniable good looks.

There was a kind of arrogance about him which appealed to many women and which Delphine found very much more exciting than the humble devotion of her previous lovers.

She always had the feeling, and it was a challenge, that she was very much more in love with the Duke than he was with her.

That she used every wile, every sophistication, that she had ever learnt, combined with an expertise which came from long practise, and still could not be sure of him made the chase even more exciting!

Delphine was determined that sooner or later he would become her abject slave, like all those upon whom she had previously bestowed her favours.

"Will Your Ladyship wear the emeralds tonight?" her maid asked.

Delphine started.

She had been staring at herself for so long in the mirror that she had for the moment forgotten where she was and what she was doing.

"The emeralds, Maria!" she said. "And that reminds me—there will be a young lady coming to stay here and she will be arriving on Friday."

"On Friday, M'Lady?"

"That is what I said," the Countess answered. "She will occupy the bed-room at the back. It will be quieter for her there than the room next door to this."

"It's very small, M'Lady."

"That will not matter," the Countess said loftily. "People who come from the country, Maria, are not used to the noise of the London traffic, and as you well know the room beside mine overlooks the street."

"Yes, of course, M'Lady, I didn't think of that."

"We must do everything to make Miss Forthingdale comfortable," the Countess said.

As she spoke she thought with satisfaction of several hostesses she knew who had daughters who had just made their début.

Tomorrow she would call on all of them and persuade them to include Anthea in their parties and take her to many of the entertainments to which they were escorting their own daughters.

"That will leave me free," the Countess said to herself. "Free to be with Garth."

She gave a little sigh of satisfaction. Then as the maid fixed the emerald tiara on her red hair she told herself that he was hers, completely and absolutely hers, as she was sure he had never belonged to another woman.

'And why not?' she thought with a little sigh of satisfaction. 'I am far more beautiful than any of them!'

Chapter Two

Anthea arrived in London in a luxury which was a vivid contrast to the discomfort of the first part of the journey.

Lady Forthingdale had at first been horrified at the idea of Anthea travelling alone to Eaton Socom.

She declared it would be impossible unless Anthea went by Post Chaise and they could find someone to accompany her.

"You are forgetting, Mama," Anthea said, "that such a way of travelling would be extremely expensive. To hire a Post Chaise for me alone would cost an astronomical amount."

Lady Forthingdale knew this was true and when she did not reply Anthea said firmly:

"I shall go by Stage Coach and I assure you I shall be very well chaperoned by the dozen or so of my fellow-passengers."

"But I do not . . ." Lady Forthingdale began, only to be silenced when Anthea said firmly:

"Either that, Mama, or I cannot afford to go to London at all. You know you have left all money matters in my hands, and I assure you it will be very difficult to find the fare even as it is."

Only when she was alone with Thais did Anthea talk about clothes and cry despairingly:

"I know exactly what you are going to say, Thais, but I cannot afford to buy myself even one more gown unless you are all to go hungry."

"Perhaps your God-mother will be generous enough to provide you with something to wear," Thais suggested.

Anthea smiled.

"We can pray she will do that, but of course I must not drop even the slightest hint of my fervent hopes. It would be far too pushing!"

Thais laughed.

"Take some of your old frocks which you wear in the garden and which are patched. That should bring it to her notice, if nothing else does!"

"I have a feeling, Thais, that you would fare far better in London than I shall," Anthea said. "Supposing you go in my place?"

"No, of course not!" Thais said. "And besides, the Countess is not my God-mother."

"It seems extraordinary," Anthea said reflectively, "that after all these years she should be so pleased to hear from Mama and so kind as to have me to stay with her."

"Mama says: 'Once a friend—always a friend.'"

"I know," Anthea replied, "but we seem to have been sadly lacking in them since Papa was killed."

"I know this house was cheap," Thais said with a little sigh, "and that is why Mama bought it. But you have to admit, Anthea, it is a dead-and-alive hole. Why, you even have to travel three miles to get to the main road where the Stage Coach passes."

This was true and Anthea could not gainsay it.

It only confirmed her determination that somehow she must save the girls from wasting their attractions and never being seen by anyone but the villagers.

It was therefore with a feeling that she was setting out on an extremely important adventure that Anthea left home the following morning, knowing she had a very long journey ahead of her.

Thais and Chloe drove her in the ancient carriage pulled by Dobbin, which was their only conveyance, to the cross-roads where the Stage Coaches to Harrogate passed once a day.

The Coach was not full and Anthea obtained an inside seat without any difficulty.

She passed the next fifteen miles chatting to a local farmer who had known her father and was only too pleased to have someone to whom he could air his grievances.

These concerned the disgraceful manner in which the Government, now that the war was over, was treating the farming community.

"They wanted us—we were important when 'Nappy' was making threatening noises just across the Channel," the farmer said bitterly, "but now that he's beat, we're beat too! Nobody is interested in us any longer."

Anthea tried to be consoling, but she was in fact glad when she reached Harrogate and could change her conveyance for a more important-looking Stage Coach. It was almost full, so she was fortunate to get a seat.

She was, however, squeezed between a fat woman with a squealing child and an elderly invalid who insisted on having both the windows up.

Before they reached the Posting-Inn where they were to rest for the night, Anthea had nursed the child, retrieved a number of ducklings which had escaped from a basket in which they were being carried to market, and listened to the invalid denouncing the expense of a treatment in Harrogate.

She also found the Coach insufferably hot and very uncomfortable.

She was in consequence so tired that she slept peacefully on the hard bed which was provided at the Posting-Inn.

Having passed an undisturbed night, she was the only passenger who was bright and smiling at the hurried breakfast served by a tired and surly waitress at five-thirty A.M. the following morning.

All this made the comfort and attention which was waiting for her at the White Horse at Eaton Socom more delightful.

The Abigail whom her God-mother had sent to meet her was not, as she had feared, an elderly and perhaps disagreeable maid who would look down her nose at a young lady from the country.

Instead, she was greeted by Emma, a girl of not more than twenty-two who was obviously excited at being entrusted with such an important mission.

"Miss Parsons, that's the head housemaid, Miss, always gets carriage-sick; so she works herself into such a fever when Her Ladyship said she was to come to meet you that she was a-shaking like a leaf—she was really!"

"I am sorry that I have caused such a commotion," Anthea smiled.

" 'Twas a bit of luck for me, Miss," Emma said. "I feels like a real Lidy, coming all this way in a slap-up carriage. I've never been in one before."

It was quite obvious that Emma was a chatter-box and, while Anthea was too tired the night she arrived at the White Horse to talk to anyone, she was quite prepared to listen as they set off for London the next morning.

Emma, sitting opposite her on the small seat of the well-padded carriage, seldom drew breath.

"I have never been to London," Anthea confided.

"It's a awful big city, Miss," Emma replied. "But there's lots of gaieties and entertainments for everyone, high or low, and 'tis not surprising that Her Lidyship likes it better'n Sheldon."

She saw that Anthea was listening attentively and went on:

"We was actually packing, Miss. The trunks had been a-brought down from the attics when your mother's letter arrives. I was helping Miss Maria, that's Her Lidyship's maid, and Her Lidyship rushes into the room crying: 'We're saved, Maria! We're saved! Unpack the trunks! We are staying in London! Oh, Maria, I am so thankful!' "

Anthea was surprised.

At the same time, she thought here was the explanation of why her mother's letter had received so quick a reply.

"Her Ladyship does not like the country?" she ventured, not wishing to appear inquisitive.

"She hates it, Miss. We all knows that, and 'tis not surprising. I've heard her say that Sheldon Castle's like a prison, and that's what it looks like, besides being miles from anywhere."

"And you too like London?" Anthea asked.

"I've got me reasons," the maid said coyly.

"You mean you have a young man."

"How did you know, Miss?" Emma asked. "He's ever so nice, but he works in London and if I had to go with Her Lidyship to Sheldon it's ten to one he'd find someone else. You can't leave a man lying about like that with no-one to look after him!"

Emma's chatter told Anthea quite a lot before they arrived.

It was obvious that the excuse of chaperoning her God-child had been very welcome to the Countess, and she also gathered that there was a profusion of Balls, parties, and other festivities to enjoy on her arrival.

She could not help feeling a little worried when she knew how few clothes her trunk strapped to the back of the travelling-carriage contained.

She had brought with her her own new gown and also Thais's best and two of her mother's. They had sat up late altering the waists and shortening the hems.

All Lady Forthingdale's daughters could sew well. Their old Nurse had seen to that, and thanks to Nanny's teaching they could copy a pattern quite skilfully from the latest magazines which showed the most elegant *toilettes* for every type of occasion.

The only difficulty was that, judging by the sketches, the austerity of the gowns worn during the war had given way to much more elaborate fashions.

Now the skirts were scalloped with lace or frills, sometimes caught up with bunches of flowers, and bodices, while still décolleté and high-waisted, were decorated in the same manner.

Anthea knew the gowns she had brought with her were pretty and undoubtedly became her. At the same time, they were very plain and of course made of the cheapest possible materials.

"Perhaps nobody will notice me," she told herself, then realised that that was in fact the last thing she wanted.

It was important that she should be noticed, and even more important that she should be admired by at least one eligible bachelor.

She wondered what sort of gentlemen her God-mother would invite to the house to meet her, and she was to find the answer to this the very night she arrived.

It was late in the afternoon when the travelling-carriage reached Sheldon House in Curzon Street.

It was an impressive mansion despite the fact that it did not stand, as Anthea had somehow expected, in a garden of its own.

The porticoed front door opened directly onto the street, but as soon as Anthea saw the fine Hall with its marble floor and curving staircase she knew that it was grander than any house she had previously visited.

She was shown into a Salon which struck her as extremely elegant and luxurious beyond her imagination of the house in which her God-mother would live.

She gazed round the room at the inlaid furniture, the exquisite *objets d'art* of gold and enamel, the Sèvres china, and the fine portraits on the walls of previous Earls and Countesses of Sheldon.

Then the Butler announced from the doorway that Her Ladyship was resting but would like Miss Forthingdale to come upstairs to her *Boudoir*.

By this time Anthea was feeling over-awed and nervous—a feeling that was not assuaged when she entered the *Boudoir* and saw her God-mother.

She had known that the Countess of Sheldon was younger than her mother but not by very many years. So she had expected her to be getting on into middle-age, in fact someone well past the lissomness of youth.

Her first glance at the Countess told her how mistaken she had been.

Lying on a *chaise longue* and wearing a diaphanous and very revealing négligée of emerald-green gauze, she appeared to Anthea to be little older than she was herself.

Never had she imagined that any woman could be so alluring!

Then as she drew nearer to her God-mother she felt embarrassed at the transparency of her négligée, revealing a slim, exquisitely curved body which it seemed impossible could belong to anyone over the age of twenty.

"Anthea, my dear child!" Delphine Sheldon said,

holding out both her hands. "It is delightful to see you! I hope you have not had too exhausting a journey?"

Anthea curtseyed, then advanced to take the soft white hands in hers.

"It is so kind of you to have me, God-mama," she said.

"I am pleased—I really am," the Countess said. "But it is very remiss of your mother not to have written to me before, and I am afraid I had forgotten that you would now be grown up. So you must forgive me!"

Two green eyes looked up in the most charming manner into Anthea's face. At the same time, she felt they were taking in every detail of her appearance.

"You are pretty, Anthea," the Countess said after a moment, "but not as lovely as your mother was at your age."

"I take after my Papa," Anthea said, "but Thais and Phebe look exactly like Mama, and they have her fair hair and blue eyes."

"I thought, when I was fifteen, that your mother was the most beautiful person I had ever seen," the Countess said.

There was no doubt, Anthea thought to herself, that her God-mother was the most beautiful person she could have imagined.

Never had she thought any woman could have such vivid red hair, such attractive green eyes slanting at the corners, and such a provocative red mouth.

"You must tell me all about your family," the Countess said, "but later, after you have rested and changed for dinner. I have arranged a party tonight in your honour, and afterwards I will take you to Almack's."

"Tonight?" Anthea asked breathlessly.

"Why not?" the Countess enquired. "The sooner you are launched into the Social World, the better! I have managed to obtain a voucher for you from my dear friend the Princess Esterhazy. I assure you, Anthea, it is very exceptional for a girl to receive one of these much-coveted vouchers the moment she arrives in London."

"I am very grateful, God-mama."

She thought that the Countess stiffened before saying:

"I have been thinking, Anthea, what you should call me. God-mama sounds quite old, almost like Grandmama, and Aunt is nearly as bad!"

Anthea waited and the Countess continued:

"I think therefore it would be best if you called me Cousin Delphine. Cousins can be any age, can they not?"

"Yes, of course," Anthea agreed.

"Your Mama and I might easily have been related. We were so close to each other and our parents' houses were adjacent. So that is the solution."

"Yes, of course," Anthea said.

"Then Cousin Delphine it is, and do not forget."

"I will remember," Anthea promised.

The Countess rang a little gold bell which stood beside her *chaise longue*.

The door was opened almost immediately by her lady's-maid.

"This is Miss Forthingdale, Maria," the Countess said. "Take her to her room. I expect the maids will have unpacked for her by now."

"Yes, M'Lady," Maria answered.

"Then good-bye, Anthea. We will meet before dinner in the Salon. Wear your prettiest gown, and remember, first impressions are always important."

Anthea was to remember her God-mother's words later in the evening when she was at Almack's and realised that she was without question the worst-dressed girl in the room.

At dinner her appearance had not seemed to matter as nobody paid any attention to her. But she was well aware that on the dance-floor her plain white muslin with one frill was conspicuously inadequate as a Ball-gown.

The gauzes, satins, silks, lamés, lawns, batistes, and tulles were all embroidered with gold and silver tinsel and bestrewn with lace, motifs, flowers, and ruches.

Each gown was a work of art, and the tiny puff-sleeves were as elaborate as the skirts.

It was little wonder that Anthea felt like a charity-child from an Institution.

"I am a country mouse," she told herself, "and no-one could mistake me for anything else."

The dinner-party had consisted of twenty exquisitely bejewelled and expensively garbed ladies and gentlemen, all of whom obviously knew one another well and, Anthea gathered, were close friends of her Godmother.

She was introduced to them all, but the Countess omitted to mention their names, while she was presented as a cousin who had come to London for what was left of the Season.

The gentlemen bowed, and the ladies gave her a condescending nod before resuming the conversation they were having before being interrupted.

At dinner Anthea had a good-looking, youngish man on one side of her who from the moment they sat down was deep in conversation with the lady on his left.

As she frequently called him "darling" in a soft, purring tone, Anthea gathered they were closely acquainted.

On her other side was a red-faced, jovial Peer who talked throughout the meal with a man two places away from him about racing.

Apparently both had horses in training and were rivals for the Gold Cup at Ascot, although Anthea gathered there were several other competitors to challenge them.

As neither of her partners spoke more than two or three words to her, she was able to observe the rest of the company with interest.

She was in fact memorising everything that she heard and saw so that she could relate it to her sisters.

"Do not forget a single thing that happens!" Chloe had admonished before she left. "You know we want to hear every detail, who the people were, what they looked like, how they dressed, and of course what they said."

"If I write it all down it will be as long as a book," Anthea said.

"Write as much as you can," Thais begged, "and store the rest in your mind."

"I will do that," Anthea promised.

She had already rehearsed to herself as she travelled in the Stage Coach how she would make her sisters laugh when she impersonated the passengers—the querulous invalid, the woman with the baby, and the farmer's wife who had inadvertently let loose the ducklings.

Looking round the dining-table, she began to see that it would be easy for her to portray some of her God-mother's guests.

She thought that she would also make little sketches of some of them on the letters which she was determined to write home at every opportunity.

Never had she seen such silver ornaments, so many flunkeys, so much glitter and expensive jewellery, or such low-cut gowns.

At the Balls she had attended in the country the gowns worn by the lady guests had not been transparent, nor had their décolletages been anything but discreet.

It seemed to Anthea that her God-mother was wearing a gown that was just as revealing as the négligée in which she had rested in her *Boudoir,* and when some of the other ladies bent forward she felt herself blushing to see how much their ample charms were disclosed.

But it was really the gentlemen who intrigued her most.

They were so much smarter and so very much more impressive than any men she had ever met before. There was no doubt that black knee-length breeches and high, meticulously tied cravats were exceedingly becoming.

She was well aware that her God-mother was "doing her proud," as her father would have said.

Almack's was the most severely exclusive and most despotically controlled Club in the whole of London. As she had read:

> Many diplomatic arts, much finesse, and a host of intrigues are set in motion to get an invitation to Almack's. Persons engaged in Commerce have no hope of ever setting foot inside the strongly guarded door.

"I will see everyone of importance," Anthea told herself when after dinner the party set off from Curzon Street.

A procession of carriages conveyed the Countess's guests, drawn by Thoroughbred horses which made Anthea long to have a closer look at them.

She found herself seated beside her God-mother in a carriage which struck her as being smarter and more luxurious than any of the others.

She was also quite certain after only a quick glimpse that the two horses which drew it could not be excelled by any other animals in the street.

It was only as they drove along that she learnt that the carriage did not belong to her God-mother, but to the gentleman who accompanied them.

"It is a long time since I have been to Almack's," he remarked. "I had hoped that I should never have to be bored again by the autocratic pretensions of its hostesses."

"Now, Garth, do not be difficult!" the Countess begged. "You know that I have to take Anthea there so that she can meet 'The Town,' and if we do not attend tonight's Ball, we shall have to wait a week for the next."

She turned to Anthea.

"Everything depends, my dear, on your making a good impression on Lady Castlereagh, Lady Jersey, Lady Cowper, the Princess de Lieven, and, of course, my dear friend the Princess Esterhazy."

"I hope I shall do that," Anthea said a little nervously.

"As the Duke has said, they are very autocratic."

Anthea started.

She had not realised that the gentleman sitting opposite her was a Duke, and she thought how thrilled the girls would be to know she had met one.

She looked at him in the lights that shone through the carriage windows as they drove up Berkeley Street.

He was, she decided, the best-looking man she had ever seen, and yet there was something about him that she felt was rather repressive.

She had not noticed him before dinner among the number of other gentlemen to whom her God-mother had introduced her.

Now she realised that he had a great distinction and an air of consequence which was unmistakable.

'He certainly looks like a Duke,' she thought to herself.

"Perhaps you will meet the Duke of Wellington," Chloe had said before she left home. "If you do, ask him if he remembers Papa."

"I shall never meet anyone half so important or so grand," Anthea replied, "and if I do, I shall be far too nervous to ask questions."

This was not the Duke of Wellington, but probably, Anthea thought, his was an older title and that was the explanation for his aloofness and a pride which was very obvious even when he was not speaking.

"How long shall we have to stay?" the Duke enquired.

"No longer than I can help," the Countess replied, "and I hope, Garth, you will ask me to dance. I am wearing a new gown especially so that I can show it off in a Ball-Room that is not as crowded as the one we were in last night."

The Duke did not answer, and after a moment the Countess said:

"You must not fail me tonight, and remember we owe so much to Anthea."

Anthea turned her head to look wide-eyed at her God-mother.

She could not understand, and when she was about to ask a question she saw the Countess hold out one hand towards the Duke.

He raised it to his lips.

"Have I ever failed you?" he asked in a low voice.

"Never!" she replied.

It was quite obvious to Anthea that for the moment they had forgotten her very existence and she kept silent. But she was listening with intense curiosity.

Almack's was all she had expected.

The large Ball-Room lit by huge crystal chandeliers, the long windows draped with elegant pelmets, the gilt-framed mirrors, and the Band high above the dancers on a special balcony were all just as she had imagined them.

There were also the Dowagers and their charges seated on gilt chairs round the room, and the hostesses introducing prospective partners to the girls, who immediately after the dance was over were returned to their Chaperons.

Princess Esterhazy greeted Anthea charmingly and, having found her two dance partners, obviously felt she had done her duty.

After dancing with a dull and unresponsive young man who was obviously not interested in her, Anthea found herself seated beside her God-mother, who was conversing with the Duke.

She watched the dancers and realised that while some of them were proficient and graceful, others were clumsy and almost grotesque in their movements.

She was so busy observing all she saw that it was with a start of surprise that she heard a voice say beside her:

"Who are you? Why have I not seen you before?"

She turned her head to see an elderly gentleman with white hair and a deeply lined face. But his dark eyes were shrewd and there was the suspicion of a twist to his thin lips.

"Because I have not been here before," Anthea replied.

"This is your first time?"

"I arrived in London this afternoon."

The old gentleman had an ivory-handled stick on which he rested a blue-veined hand.

One leg was stuck out in front of him and Anthea thought he must be lame.

He was, however, most elegantly dressed, although perhaps he was slightly old-fashioned in that he was wearing a fob and there was a large diamond ring on one of his fingers.

Anthea had read somewhere that Beau Brummell, when he was the arbiter of fashion, had declared that for a man jewellery was in bad taste, and that therefore none of the Bucks and Dandies surrounding the Regent wore any jewellery.

"So you are congratulating yourself," the old gentleman said, "that you have entered the holy of holies."

"I am thinking how lucky I am," Anthea answered.

"I do not know that there is much luck about it," her companion growled, "unless you are referring to the fortunes of birth. The colour of your blood gets you in here—talents are not considered an asset."

Anthea laughed.

"I am glad about that."

"Are you telling me you have no talents?"

"Not many," Anthea confessed, remembering her conversation with her sisters.

"A good thing, too!" the old gentleman said positively. "Far too many women today are trying to push themselves forward. All I ask is that a woman should be a woman. I have always liked them that way."

He glanced at Anthea in what she thought was a mischievous manner.

Because she liked him she said impulsively:

"Would it be very rude, Sir, if I asked you to tell me who some of the people are? You see, I want to know about them so that I can tell my sisters when I get home."

The old gentleman chuckled.

"If you keep your ears open while you are in London you will have plenty to repeat," he said. "What is your name, young lady?"

"Anthea Forthingdale, Sir."

"I am the Marquess of Chale."

Anthea gave a little gasp.

"I think I have heard of you, Sir."

"And nothing to my advantage, I'll be bound!" the Marquess said. "If you want to know who these creatures are—there is one that will amuse you!"

He pointed out a rather heavily built man who was dancing energetically with a very pretty woman wearing an egret in her hair.

"That is Alvanley," he said. "He has plenty of wit and enjoys two things."

"What are they?" Anthea asked.

"Gambling and cold apricot tart!"

Anthea looked at him to see if he was joking.

"It is true!" the Marquess said. "He once found an apricot tart so delectable that he ordered his Chef to have one on the side-board every day throughout the year."

"How extraordinary!" Anthea exclaimed.

"A popular fellow, but a nuisance to his hosts and hostesses when he stays with them."

"Why is that?"

"They always have to order one of their servants to sit up all night outside his bed-room."

"Whatever for?"

"After reading late, he extinguishes his candle either by throwing it on the floor, aiming a pillow at it, or pushing it, still alight, under the bolster!"

Anthea laughed.

"Is that really true?"

"It is indeed!" the Marquess said. "If you intend to observe Society you might as well learn of their eccentricities."

"Tell me more," Anthea begged.

"See that chap?"

The Marquess pointed with his stick at a handsome man with bold dark eyes, dancing with a pretty girl who was however on the fat side.

"Colonel Dan McKinnon—a great jokester," the Marquess said. "Notorious for practical jokes!"

"What sort of jokes?"

"Once, in Spain, he impersonated the Duke of

York and kept it up, with the connivance of his Regi-
mental friends, for several hours."

"What happened?"

"When a huge bowl of punch was served by the
Mayor at a Banquet given in his honour, he suddenly
dove into it, throwing his heels into the air!"

Anthea laughed again.

"You make everyone sound very funny!"

"They are, if you watch people, as I do. I'll tell
you another story about Colonel McKinnon. He is a
favourite with your sex. Women go mad about him,
but they soon bore him and when he leaves them they
weep their eyes out."

"I can understand that," Anthea said.

She thought that Colonel McKinnon with his dark
eyes and athletic figure was unusually attractive.

"One lady," the Marquess went on, "wrote Mc-
Kinnon a letter full of reproaches. She threatened sui-
cide and demanded the return of a lock of her hair she
had given him."

"Did he return it to her?"

"He sent his orderly with a large packet containing
several locks of hair ranging from blonde to red, from
black to grey. With it was a message—'Pick out your
own!' "

"That was cruel!" Anthea cried.

The Marquess was obviously pleased to have an
audience and he continued to chatter on, telling Anthea
stories which she knew would enthrall the girls.

The Duchess of York, she learnt, had an obsession
for dogs that was making her look ridiculous.

At one time she had a hundred, many of them
rather dirty, sharing her apartment.

A man called Akers—Anthea never learnt if he
had a title or not—who enjoyed driving a four-in-hand,
had had his front teeth filed, and paid fifty guineas to
"Hell-Fire Dick," the driver of the Cambridge Tele-
graph Coach, to teach him to spit in the familiar coachman style!

Anthea was so enthralled with what the Marquess
was saying that she did not realise that the Countess,

at whose side she was sitting, had risen to dance with the Duke.

As they passed by, the Marquess looked at them and said:

"That is the Countess of Sheldon—devilishly attractive woman, but hot to the touch. I imagine Sheldon has a hard time keeping her within bounds."

Anthea was not certain what this meant, so she was silent as the Marquess continued:

"Well, she will have met her match with Axminster! He is another who leaves a trail of broken hearts behind him."

"He looks very proud," Anthea ventured.

"Got something to be proud about!" the Marquess retorted. "Ancient family, great wealth! They have all tried to catch him, but the betting in White's is that they will fail."

"You mean—girls want to marry him?" Anthea asked.

"That is right, but he likes them already married and sophisticated. Who shall blame him? And it is safer, unless the husband turns nasty."

Anthea watched her God-mother and the Duke with renewed interest.

From what the Marquess was suggesting, it sounded as if the Duke was in love with the Countess.

Then she told herself that the married women her mother knew all behaved with the utmost circumspection. If people were saying unkind things, it was undoubtedly a piece of malicious gossip because her God-mother was so beautiful.

She was wondering whether she ought to reveal to the Marquess that she was in fact staying with the lady he had just described as "devilishly attractive" when the Countess stopped dancing and came across the room to Anthea.

"Dearest child," she said, "I have been most remiss in not finding you a partner. The Duke would be delighted if you would finish this dance with him."

"Oh, no!" Anthea tried to protest.

But the Countess moved away and the Duke put

his arm round Anthea and without speaking started to waltz.

She was fortunately not afraid of disgracing herself on the dance-floor, having practised the waltz with her sisters and always been in demand at local Balls.

At the same time, she had never danced with anyone as important as a Duke, and she looked up at him from under her eye-lashes hoping he would not find her too countryfied or not proficient enough to follow his lead.

She realised with some consternation that he was in fact looking extremely bored.

There was no misunderstanding the expression on his face and she was sure as he swung her round the room that he had been forced by her God-mother into dancing with her against his will.

Because her mother had always said that silence was boring and people should try to make polite conversation whoever they were with, Anthea said after a moment:

"The Marquess of Chale was telling me the most interesting things about some of the people here."

"I should not believe more than half he tells you," the Duke replied coldly. "His Lordship is known as the most inveterate gossip in the whole of White's!"

Anthea knew that this was the most important Gentlemen's Club in London, and she remembered hearing that the Dandies lounged in a bow-window, eyeing the women passing in the street and making rude remarks about them.

She would have liked to ask the Duke about White's, but there had been something crushing in the manner in which he had spoken of the Marquess.

She thought to herself that it was obviously an effort for him not only to dance with her, but also to converse with anyone so unimportant.

It was therefore with a sense of relief that she heard the Band stop playing and realised that the dance was over.

The Duke took her back to her God-mother, moving so swiftly that it was in itself an insult. Very different, Anthea thought, from the languid way in which he had moved while dancing.

"I hope you enjoyed your dance," the Countess said as they joined her. "After all, it is not every débutante who has the privilege of dancing with a Duke the very first night she makes an appearance at Almack's."

She glanced up at the Duke with a mischievous twinkle in her eyes as she added:

"I am sure you would like to stand up with Anthea in the Quadrille."

"I think it is time for me to return home," the Duke said. "I do not like keeping my horses out late."

He spoke sharply and Anthea fancied there was an almost defiant look in his eyes as he met the Countess's.

Just for a moment it seemed as if it was a battle of wills, then she capitulated.

"It *is* getting late, Garth," she agreed, "and Anthea has had a long day. I am sure she has seen all she wants of Almack's."

They said good-night to the Princess Esterhazy, Anthea thanking Her Highness prettily for having been her sponsor.

"It has been a pleasure, Miss Forthingdale," she said, "and you must persuade your cousin to bring you here again next week."

"I shall try to do so, Ma'am," Anthea answered.

There was a great deal of curtseying, and a large number of gentlemen seemed to wish to kiss the Countess's hand before finally they were outside and stepping into the Duke's carriage.

As they drove back to Curzon Street, neither the Duke nor the Countess seemed to have much to say.

As they stepped out onto the pavement the Countess held out her hand to the Duke and said:

"I thank Your Grace for your kindness to me and to my guest. We are both very grateful."

Anthea curtseyed. They went into the house, and the Butler who had let them in stood at the open door until the Duke's carriage drove away.

"We will go straight up to bed, Dawson," the Countess said as he closed the front door. "As His

Lordship is not here, there is no need to leave a foot-man on duty in the Hall tonight."

"Thank you, Your Ladyship," the Butler said. "James will be very grateful for your consideration."

The Countess smiled at him and started up the stairs.

"Come along, Anthea," she said. "You need your beauty sleep and I have a great many delightful things planned for you tomorrow."

"You are very kind," Anthea answered. "I cannot tell you how grateful I am and how thrilling it was to visit Almack's this evening."

"I can see I am going to enjoy having you here," the Countess said.

They reached the top of the stairs and she moved her head forward, obviously inviting Anthea to kiss her cheek.

"Sleep well, dear child," she said. "There will be no reason for you to hurry in the morning. I never breakfast before ten o'clock."

As she spoke, she moved away towards her bed-room and Anthea saw that her maid, Maria, was wait-ing for her.

Emma too must have heard their arrival, for she came hurrying into the bed-room almost as soon as Anthea reached it.

"Did you have a nice time, Miss?" she asked.

"I had a lovely time, Emma!" Anthea replied. "And Almack's was all I expected it to be."

"The ladies at dinner had very fine gowns," Emma enthused. "We was all peeping over the banisters when the company left and we thought the jewellery alone must be worth a fortune!"

"I thought that too," Anthea replied.

It only took a short time to put on her nightgown and brush her hair. As soon as Emma left her she got into bed.

She thought she would fall asleep the moment her head touched the pillow, but instead she found herself remembering everything that had happened, all the people she had met, and what the Marquess had told her.

"I must not forget anything," she said to herself.

An hour later she was still awake.

She got up and, lighting the candle by her bed, looked round for a piece of paper.

"I will write down the names," she said, and wondered how one spelt "Alvanley."

Her room was too small to contain a writing-desk, and unfortunately when she had come away she had left in such a hurry that she had not brought a writing-pad or even her sketching-book with her.

She had however packed her paint-box and several pencils, but they were no use without paper to write on.

She remembered that she had noticed in the Salon when she was waiting to be shown upstairs to her God-mother's *Boudoir* a very elegant Louis XIV *secrétaire* standing in one of the windows.

It had been open and she had seen on it a blotter embellished with the Sheldon coat-of-arms, and a silver rack containing the thick white vellum paper on which the Countess had written to her mother.

"I will go downstairs and get some," Anthea decided.

She put on a wrap over her nightgown, and thinking she would be quieter if she moved bare-foot, she did not bother to put on the slippers which Emma had arranged beside a chair in her room.

She opened her door quietly.

The house was very quiet. There were only two or three candles alight in the silver sconces in the Hall and on the stairs, but they gave enough light for Anthea to find her way without difficulty.

She reached the Salon and found that by leaving the door open she was able to find her way to the *secrétaire*.

As she had suspected, there was plenty of paper in the silver rack and she took several sheets.

As she would doubtless awaken long before her hostess, she thought she would write a long letter to the girls, telling them all that had happened to date.

She came from the Salon and as she did so she heard a sound at the front door.

She stood still, thinking she must have been mistaken. Then it came again and it seemed as if someone was interfering with the lock.

Thoughts of burglars and robbers swept through Anthea's mind and she wondered whether she should scream or run for help.

She had an idea that the servants slept in the basement, but she was not sure.

She had seen only the first two floors since her arrival and had no idea where the men-servants' quarters might be.

Then the front door opened and a man came into the house.

He turned round to shut the door behind him and as Anthea stood watching, feeling as if she were paralysed and could neither move nor make a sound, he turned towards the stairs.

To her complete and utter astonishment she saw that it was the Duke!

At the same time as she recognised him, he saw her standing in her white wrapper staring at him.

"What are you doing here?" he asked sharply.

"I . . . I thought you were a . . . burglar!" she faltered. "I was . . . just going to . . . scream!"

There was a moment's silence. Then the Duke said:

"I remembered something—important that I had to tell—Her Ladyship."

Anthea walked towards him.

"C-Cousin Delphine has retired. If it is . . . important, I could . . . take her a message."

The Duke was standing with one foot on the stairs.

In the dim light of the flickering candles he looked very large and overpowering.

"I will convey the message," he said after a moment.

"But . . . Cousin Delphine is in . . . bed," Anthea insisted.

Again there was a pause before the Duke with a note of amusement in his voice said:

"My good girl, go to bed yourself and do not interfere in other people's affairs."

He did not wait for a reply.

He walked up the stairs as he spoke and on reaching the landing turned in the direction of the Countess's room and disappeared from sight.

Anthea stood staring after him.

Then as the full implication of what he had said and what he was doing swept over her, the colour rose in a crimson tide up her pale face.

Chapter Three

Anthea was both shocked and embarrassed.

Although she had read the passionate love-poems which interested her mother, she had never mentally translated them into actual physical activity.

The fact that the Duke was, as she now realised, the lover of her God-mother seemed to her to be shocking and an outrage against decency.

She had never imagined that older people, or rather women of her mother's age, would have the type of liaison that she connected with the Kings of France or Charles II.

They had just seemed to be mythical figures which had no real semblance of humanity about them.

To be confronted with the fact that her God-mother was having a clandestine affair with the Duke of Axminster was a revelation which exploded in her mind like a bombshell.

She also felt very ignorant, and the blush which had suffused her face when the Duke told her not to interfere in other people's affairs seemed to burn its way into her consciousness all through the night.

If she could have had a choice, Anthea, when morning came, would have sped back to Yorkshire to hide herself amongst the familiar objects she knew and understood.

She wondered frantically whether the Duke had told her God-mother what had occurred.

She was in fact sure he had done so when at nine-thirty A.M., half an hour earlier than her God-mother usually was called, she was summoned to the Countess's bedroom.

As Anthea walked along the passage she tried to think of what she could say, what explanation she could make, but could only feel that being gauche and countryfied was hardly an excuse for making such a *bêtise*.

The Countess, looking more alluring than ever, was propped up against a profusion of lace-edged pillows, her red hair falling over her shoulders, her eyes very green in the morning light.

Anthea stood just inside the doorway, wondering apprehensively what her God-mother would say, and was surprised when the Countess said with a smile on her red lips:

"Good-morning, Anthea. I thought you might like to drive with me in the Park this morning, and after that I feel we should visit Bond Street and see if there is some little object which takes your fancy and which I might give you as a present."

Even as she spoke Anthea realised she was being bribed.

It affronted her pride and her self-respect that her God-mother should think for one moment that she could not be trusted to be discreet without an inducement to keep her lips closed.

She was just about to reply that there was nothing she needed when the Countess gave a cry so shrill and sharp that Anthea was startled.

"Is that the best gown you have?" she asked. "And I noticed the one you wore last night! Oh, Anthea, how remiss of me! How inexcusable that I should not have thought of it!"

"Thought of . . . what, Cousin Delphine?" Anthea asked, bewildered.

"That you would need new gowns coming to London from Yorkshire, and I forgot too that your father was not wealthy. How could I have been so negligent?"

Without giving time for Anthea to answer, the

Countess picked up the bell beside her bed and rang it violently.

When Maria ran in she exclaimed:

"Why could you not have told me, Maria, that Miss Forthingdale required new gowns! We knew she was coming from the country. I am mortified that we have been so obtuse as not to have had some ready for her."

"I do not . . . wish to be a . . . nuisance . . ." Anthea began, only to have anything she might have said swept to one side!

Her God-mother imperiously commanded Maria to bring from the wardrobes everything that she did not need and which could be altered immediately.

"I will buy you some new gowns," the Countess said, "but they will of course take time. What we must do in the meanwhile is to contrive that you look fashionable and well-dressed in my clothes, and there are in fact plenty for which I have no further use."

This was an understatement, Anthea found an hour later, when she was being presented with dozens of gowns all so smart, so exquisitely made, that she could not understand how her God-mother could bear to part with them. But the Countess had a valid excuse for everything she gave away.

Maria would hold up a dream of sparkling gauze.

"I wore that at the Duchess of Bedford's Ball," the Countess explained. "It was the envy of every woman present, but I cannot appear in it again."

When Maria showed a dress and coat of cream satin with appliqué work of green velvet leaves, she said:

"I have worn that ensemble twice at Carlton House and the Prince Regent admired it enormously, so he will not wish to mention it another time!"

There were Ball-gowns and complete *toilettes* for the afternoon, for the morning, and for travelling.

There were high-crowned bonnets to go with them, festooned with feathers, flowers, and ribbons.

There were reticules to match the gowns and slippers dyed to the same colour, which fortunately fitted Anthea, being only just a trifle larger than her own.

She lost count of how many different garments Maria brought from the wardrobes and from another room, and yet there still seemed to be a multitude left.

All the clothes she was given, Anthea realised, were in the hues which suited the Countess best: greens to match her eyes, jonquil yellow and gold to bring out the lights of her hair, deep blue to accentuate the white of her skin.

There were also a number of white gowns which, as her God-mother pointed out, were extremely suitable for a débutante.

Anthea was too overwhelmed to realise that very many of the gowns she was given were really too sophisticated and too elaborate for a young girl.

But even when she thought later that some of them were a trifle overwhelming, they were certainly preferable to the plain muslins she had made herself.

Muslin, she learnt from Maria, was a material which had gone out of fashion since the war ended.

Some of the coats were trimmed with bands of expensive furs like ermine and sable. But when Anthea suggested humbly that she should cut them off, the Countess held up her hands in horror.

"You must not alter the style, child!" she cried. "Besides, what would I do with the strips of ermine or the lengths of sable except throw them in the wastepaper basket!"

Anthea shuddered at such extravagance!

Yet, while occasionally she protested that her God-mother was giving her too much, she could not help realising that she now had enough clothes not only to dress herself but also Thais and Chloe.

"How can I ever thank you?" she asked.

But she understood perfectly what her God-mother meant when she replied:

"You can thank me, Anthea, by being my loyal friend, as your mother was when we were young together."

"I should be honoured," Anthea managed to say politely.

At the same time, she could not help wishing that the Countess had not supposed that her silence must be bought.

In the days that followed, Anthea found that her God-mother had arranged in an extremely efficient manner that she was seldom in Sheldon House.

There were several ladies, two of whom were related to the Earl, who were introducing their own daughters to Society.

They had apparently been coerced into including Anthea in the parties, the expeditions, and the Balls to which they took their own progeny.

It was after a week of being passed from hand to hand and of associating with girls of her own age that Anthea decided that she much preferred the fascinating Social figures who made up her God-mother's particular circle.

She went with the Countess to a dinner-party which was very like the one which had taken place on the night of her arrival.

Now that she had found her feet and was not so bewildered, Anthea found the conversation exciting, witty, and informative.

It was very unlike the inanities and incessant giggling that she had to endure from the other débutantes.

What was more, she found it a delight to look at the gentlemen in her God-mother's parties.

The beardless youths who partnered the young were, she found, so half-witted that she had to force herself to be polite to them.

Fortunately, even though she dined with her young acquaintances, they afterwards attended the Balls given by the great political or Social hostesses.

There Anthea invariably found the Marquess of Chale.

"I have something amusing to tell you, Miss Forthingdale," he would say as soon as she appeared.

At the first opportunity she would sit beside him, listening to his anecdotes and to his often spiteful but invariably amusing tales about the people in the Ball-Room.

"I cannot think why you waste your time with

that old gossip," one of the Dowagers who was chaperoning Anthea said to her.

She would not have understood if Anthea had replied that it was the Marquess's conversation which made her letters to Yorkshire sparkle as brightly as the diamonds round her God-mother's neck.

As the Countess rose late and Anthea, however late she went to bed, could not get out of her country habit of waking early, a day seldom passed without a fat envelope being placed on the Hall-table for the Butler to frank.

Determined that her sisters should feel they were a part of her own experiences, Anthea not only described all she saw, but also drew sketches of the people she met.

She of course made no mention of the Duke's special place in her God-mother's life, but she related that she had met him and drew a picture of him looking extremely disdainful and very autocratic.

She could not help feeling shy and tense when they met, even though he behaved towards her with the same polite indifference he had shown the night of her arrival.

She told herself that he had probably never given another thought to her stupidity in not understanding why he had called at Sheldon House in the middle of the night.

But even to think of how obtuse and foolish she had been was to bring the colour to her cheeks and to increase her dislike of the Duke for having inadvertently placed her in such a humiliating position.

She learnt that he was much younger than her God-mother and in fact had only just passed his twenty-eighth birthday.

But this, she felt, did not excuse the fact that he was behaving extremely reprehensibly in pursuing another man's wife and actually making love to her in her husband's house.

There was however no doubt that, as the Marquess had said, the Countess was a "devilishly attractive woman."

Anthea used to watch the enticing manner in

which she would look at the Duke from under her long, mascaraed eye-lashes, the way she had of touching him with her soft white hands and of pouting her red lips provocatively.

She was not surprised that he could not resist such blandishments, and she found from what she had learnt in other houses that her God-mother had in fact succeeded in capturing a citadel which had resisted many other attacks upon it.

"I always thought that Axminster would marry the Duke of Brockenhurst's daughter," one Dowager remarked to another in Anthea's hearing.

"So did the Duchess!" the other replied. "But he was far too wily. They have all tried to catch him, but he confines himself to women who are already married."

"He never leaves Delphine Sheldon's side," the first Dowager said tartly.

"Are you surprised?" was the reply. "She is certainly in good looks, and she might as well make the most of what is left of her youth."

"You are too charitable, my love! Personally, it would give me a great deal of pleasure to see His Grace marched down the aisle by some determined young female. He has been a disturbing influence in the Social World for far too long!"

"All handsome, wealthy Dukes are that!" her friend laughed. "It will have to be a very early bird who finally catches Axminster!"

Because the Duke was constantly in her mind, Anthea knew without even seeing him that he was always in Sheldon House.

She longed to discuss him with the Marquess, but she realised that that would be disloyal to her God-mother, and with difficulty she contained her curiosity.

The two new gowns which the Countess ordered for her in Bond Street were pink and therefore very becoming to Anthea's dark hair.

She wore them for all really important parties and the more elaborate of them to Carlton House when she was presented to the Prince Regent.

When she rose from a deep curtsey he informed

her with the charm for which he was renowned that she was "pretty, very pretty indeed," but he doubted if she would ever eclipse her cousin, Delphine.

"I would not presume to attempt such a thing, Sire," Anthea replied.

She found to her surprise that she was not at all nervous and that in fact the Regent was not half so awe-inspiring in person as he appeared in his pictures and caricatures.

"All women want attention," he answered, "and they all wish to compete with their own sex."

"Only in an effort to capture the attention of gentlemen who are exceedingly fastidious and critical, like yourself, Sire," Anthea answered.

The Prince chuckled in delight at what she had been half-afraid he would think an impertinence.

But he had taken it as a compliment and later in the evening he singled Anthea out to show her a new picture he had recently acquired.

"You were a success with His Royal Highness," the Countess said when they were driving home. "It is a pity that that is the last party he will give. He is leaving London for Brighton next Friday."

"Does that mean it is the end of the Season?" Anthea asked.

"I am afraid so," the Countess replied with a note of regret in her voice.

"Then I . . . shall have to . . . go home."

"There is no hurry, my dear."

But three days later a letter from the Earl made it clear to his wife that he was aware of the Prince Regent's plans and that it was time for her to return to the country.

"Nothing can save us now," the Countess said miserably to the Duke.

* * *

Anthea descended from the Stage Coach at the cross-roads to find Thais and Chloe waiting for her with Dobbin.

As she walked towards them and the guard on the Stage Coach began to unload half a dozen large leather trunks, they stared at her, too astonished for the moment to say anything.

"I am home!" Anthea cried. "And oh, how thrilled I am to see you!"

Her voice was the same, there was still the same sparkle in her eyes, the same dimples in her cheeks, but otherwise it was hard to recognise the Anthea who had gone away from them.

This was someone they had never seen before, in an emerald-green travelling-gown and coat to match, with a high-brimmed bonnet trimmed with emerald-green ostrich-feathers.

"Anthea! Can it really be you?" Chloe exclaimed.

"I have never seen anything so smart, so absolutely breath-taking!" Thais cried.

The guard from the Stage Coach set the trunks down on the road-side, then accepting the tip Anthea handed him, touched his high hat respectfully and climbed back onto the box.

The Coach rumbled off and Chloe climbed from the carriage to ask excitedly:

"What is in those trunks? What have you brought, Anthea?"

"Clothes!" Anthea answered. "Gowns, all like the one I am wearing! There are dozens of them . . . dozens and dozens!"

"I cannot believe it!" Thais cried. "How can you have got them? Where did they come from?"

"God-mama gave them to me," Anthea explained. "But I have something far more important to tell you than that!"

"What is it?" Thais asked.

"We are rich!"

"Rich?"

The girls gasped and Anthea said:

"I cannot wait to tell you everything! But first let us find someone to help us with these trunks. I dare not try to lift them myself or I shall split the sleeves of my gown."

"No, no! Do not touch them!" Thais said quickly.

Several small boys were summoned and for two pennies lifted the trunks onto the carriage.

Thais turned Dobbin's head homeward and they set off moving slowly because it was quite a load for the old horse.

"What do you mean—you are rich?" Chloe asked.

"I have discovered how to make money," Anthea replied. "Oh, girls, it is so exciting! I have so much to tell you that I felt as if I should never get here. Even Her Ladyship's carriage in which she sent me to Eaton Socom seemed to crawl, though it was drawn by four horses. Think of that!"

"Tell us about the money," Chloe pleaded. "Have you won a lottery or been gambling? I cannot think—"

She stopped suddenly and said with a different note in her voice:

"You do not mean you are engaged to be married, Anthea?"

"No, no, of course not!" Anthea said. "It is something much more exciting!"

"How could it be?" Thais asked.

"It is," Anthea answered, "because I can make money myself; and what is more, I can make as much as I want, as much as we need!"

"But how? How?" Thais enquired.

"By selling my sketches!" Anthea replied.

It took Anthea some time to explain what had happened only a week before she was due to return home.

It was after her visit to Carlton House that she realised that while she had greatly enjoyed her time in London and it had been an experience which she felt had in some ways changed her outlook on life, she had not achieved what she had set out to do.

She had not found herself a husband!

Many of her partners had paid her compliments and several had flirted with her in a manner which made her think their intentions might be serious.

But she had not in fact received a single offer of marriage.

There was no doubt that after she was dressed in the latest fashion and, on her God-mother's insistence,

Maria added a touch of cosmetics to the clearness of her skin, she received quite a lot of attention.

She was never without partners at any of the Balls, and two gentlemen went so far as to try to kiss her in the garden between dances.

But while they declared that their hearts were irretrievably lost, she learnt from her friend the Marquess of Chale that both would be obliged to marry wealthy women if their Estates were to remain intact.

"The men who are wealthy enough to choose a wife without any other assets than a pretty face are few and far between," the Marquess informed her.

Anthea was well aware that he was warning her not to be too cast down at not receiving an offer.

"Besides, most of them, like Axminster," he went on, "have a very inflated idea of their own importance."

Anthea could not help feeling dispirited when she realised that when the Season was over her hour of glory would be over too.

She must return to Yorkshire, go back to scrimping and saving for the family, making one penny do the work of two, looking forward to nothing more thrilling than the local Hunt-Ball in December.

Then fate took an interest in her predicament.

She was waiting for her God-mother the next morning and as usual the Countess was late.

She had a habit, Anthea discovered, of getting completely dressed in one expensive and fascinating ensemble, then deciding she would wear something quite different and changing everything from her bonnet down to her slippers.

The carriage was outside the door and Anthea had waited for over twenty minutes in the Hall, when feeling restless she entered a room she had not seen since she had arrived at Sheldon House.

It was, she knew, the Earl's special Sanctum, and it made her think of her father because she was certain it was the sort of room he would have liked to have if he could have afforded it.

There was a deep, comfortable leather sofa and

arm-chairs to match, a huge writing-desk, and against
one wall there stood a large Chippendale bookcase with
dozens of beautiful bound books behind the glass.

Anthea moved towards them, feeling she had been
somewhat remiss in not discovering them before.

On the other walls of the room were a number of
framed caricatures and cartoons which she saw had
been done by the famous satirical artist James Gillray
and Thomas Rowlandson.

She had heard these often referred to in conversation, and she had learnt that everyone found most
amusing those which had been published recently by a
third cartoonist, George Cruikshank.

She stood staring at the drawings, seeing that they
were extremely clever and that she could easily recognise the better-known figures in them.

There was no mistaking the Prince Regent and
the ample proportions of Lady Hertford.

There were a large number of wartime cartoons
depicting Napoleon in various guises. In one by James
Gillray, he was shown as Belshazzar, seeing the writing
on the wall.

They fascinated Anthea and she went from picture
to picture.

She was just feeling disappointed because there
were no more to see, when she found a portfolio lying
on a table and realised it contained dozens of unframed
sketches.

The one on the top was a sarcastic reference to the
payment of thirty-five thousand pounds for the Elgin
marbles when John Bull and his numerous family required bread.

"That is brilliant! Really brilliant!" Anthea said
to herself, and turning over the cartoons found herself
laughing first at one, then at another.

Quite suddenly she realised that some of them
were not unlike the sketches she herself had drawn
for the girls!

'I am sure,' she thought, 'I can learn a great
deal from studying Gillray, Rowlandson, and Cruikshank.'

Rowlandson, she could see, used a reed pen and added washes of brilliant colour. His crowds, his absurd men, and his plump women showing their legs were slightly coarse.

At the same time, Anthea thought, there was a rollicking zest about his cartoons which made them very funny.

She heard her God-mother calling her and hurried into the Hall to find the Countess descending the staircase looking quite dazzling in a daffodil-coloured gown, her long white neck encircled with topazes and with feathers to match in her enormous bonnet.

"What are you doing in His Lordship's room?" she asked.

"I hope it was not wrong of me, Cousin Delphine, but I was looking at the cartoons," Anthea replied.

"Oh, the Earl collects them all! Personally I find them very tiresome and so exaggerated that it is difficult to recognise anybody."

Anthea knew this was untrue. When they drove down St. James's Street the following day she saw crowds outside Humphrey's Print Shop and guessed that a new cartoon by either Rowlandson or Cruikshank had been issued.

She questioned the Marquess the same evening about the cartoonists.

"Those fellows make a fortune!" he said. "But they make people laugh and that does nobody any harm."

"Is James Gillray still alive?" Anthea asked.

"No, he died of drink in 1811," the Marquess replied. "I have always understood that it was the terrific demand for his work that drove him to the bottle."

"I was looking at some of his drawings today."

"In the Earl's collection? He seldom misses a new one, but there are now not as many published as there used to be. Rowlandson is past his prime and is getting lazy. There is only Cruikshank, who is very young, in fact in his early twenties!"

"As young as that?" Anthea asked. "And yet people buy his cartoons?"

"People will buy anything for a good laugh," the Marquess replied.

Anthea was rather pensive for the rest of the evening.

When Emma had left her in her nightgown ready to get to bed, she took from the drawer a sketch-book she had bought since coming to London, in which she had done a number of drawings to show to her sisters.

They all portrayed the Social figures she had seen at Almack's and at the other parties.

She realised as she looked at them that she had caricatured everyone in a manner which was in fact not unlike Gillray's work.

The coloured wash she had added made her finished pictures resemble Rowlandson's and Cruikshank's.

She examined some of her sketches critically, then with a determined expression on her face she got into bed.

The next morning she rose early, before her Godmother was called, and taking Emma with her she hired a hackney-carriage and drove to 27 St. James's Street.

She left Emma outside and went in and asked for the Proprietor.

She was surprised to find that he was a she, and to meet Mrs. Humphrey, an elderly, be-spectacled lady, square-faced, with a small, tight mouth, wearing a white bonnet.

"What can I do for you, Madam?" she enquired.

Anthea felt rather shy as she produced her sketch-book.

"I am . . . wondering," she said, "whether it would be . . . possible for me . . . to sell one of these?"

She knew, as Mrs. Humphrey took the book from her, that she was calculating how she could refuse, politely and without giving offense, to buy anything.

Then as she turned over the pages her expression altered.

"Have you done these yourself?" she enquired, an incredulous note in her voice.

"Yes."

"Have you offered them to anyone else?"

"No," Anthea replied. "I drew them to amuse my sisters, who live in the country. Yesterday I was looking at some of Mr. Gillray's cartoons and I saw the name of your shop on the back."

"Mr. Gillray is a very great loss indeed."

"I am sure he must be," Anthea answered, "but I see you publish the work of Mr. George Cruikshank."

"A clever young man," Mrs. Humphrey said, "but not the artist that James Gillray was or indeed his successor, Thomas Rowlandson."

She turned some more pages of Anthea's sketchbook, then she said:

"You say you wish to sell these?"

"Are they worth anything?" Anthea asked.

"If you will excuse me a moment," Mrs. Humphrey said, "I would just like to speak to my associates."

She disappeared into the back of the shop and Anthea stood looking round her.

There were not only caricatures on the long tables but also some rather delightful water-colours, which made Anthea realise that she certainly could not compete in that field.

Mrs. Humphrey returned.

"You have not told me your name, Madam," she said.

Anthea thought quickly.

She was quite certain that it would be a mistake, if she did publish any of her caricatures, to allow anyone to know her name.

"My name is Dale," she said. "Miss Ann Dale."

"Very well, Miss Dale," Mrs. Humphrey said. "I would like to tell you that my associates and I think very highly of the sketches you have just brought me."

"You do!" Anthea exclaimed.

"We would be willing to publish them all."

"All?" Anthea questioned faintly.

She thought she could not be hearing correctly.

"You can accept payment by subscription or receive a sum of money outright for copyright."

"I am afraid I do not understand," Anthea said.

"There are two ways for an artist to sell cartoons and caricatures," Mrs. Humphrey explained. "Sometimes the artist will sell his work outright to the printer. The other way is for him to receive a small sum down and to take fifty per cent of every copy which is bought. These, as you will see if you look round the shop, are usually sold at one-sixth to two pence each. Yet a Thomas Rowlandson occasionally fetches as much as three pounds."

Anthea thought for a moment, then she said:

"If you bought my drawings outright, what would you give me for them?"

Mrs. Humphrey looked down at the sketch-book and seemed to be calculating.

Then she said:

"Seeing that we are short of cartoonists at the moment and these sketches illustrate a social angle that has not been portrayed before, I am prepared, Miss Dale, to offer you ten pounds each for them!"

For a moment Anthea thought she must be joking. Then in a voice which hardly seemed to be her own she answered:

"I would like to accept that, Mrs. Humphrey."

From that moment it seemed to her as if she was in a dream from which she was afraid she would awaken!

Even now as she told her sisters what had happened she could hardly believe it was really true.

"Ten pounds!" Chloe said in an awe-struck voice.

"How many did you sell?" Thais asked.

"There were ten in the book," Anthea replied.

"A hundred pounds!"

"It cannot be true!"

"And they will take as many more as I want to send them," Anthea said.

The burble of noise which came from Thais's and Chloe's lips made it difficult to say any more until they had travelled for at least a mile.

Then as they neared home Anthea said:

"I was thinking as I drove north that it would be a mistake for us to tell Mama. You know she would be shocked at me trading my drawings, and she would also be afraid that someone might discover my indentity."

"Yes, you are quite right," Thais said in a serious tone. "It would only worry her."

"I will just pay more of the money into the Bank," Anthea said. "I persuaded Mrs. Humphrey to give me cash."

She remembered that she had had to wait for quite a while while Mrs. Humphrey procured the hundred pounds, and she had been afraid that when she got back to the house her God-mother would ask where she had been.

She swore Emma to secrecy by saying that she had been to buy a special present for the Earl to thank him for having her to stay at Sheldon House.

This story was easily substantiated by the fact that Mrs. Humphrey had given her George Cruikshank's latest cartoon as a gift and Anthea had shown it to Emma.

"I can't make head nor tail o' them drawings," Emma said. "My young man enjoys them, but I thinks, if you asks me, Miss, a man likes a laugh more'n a woman."

"What makes you think that, Emma?" Anthea asked.

"Well, I'm always wanting to talk about love and how much we matters to each other," Emma said. "But Jim—he just wants to 'ave a good laugh. 'Come on, Em,' he says, 'yer knows I love yer. We don't have to look all gloomy abaht it.' "

Anthea, before she left London, had bought her God-mother a pretty paper-knife that she had admired in a shop in Bond Street, and asked her to convey the Cruikshank cartoon to the Earl.

"That is a very sweet thought, Anthea," the Countess had said. "I am so glad you have enjoyed your visit and you know how delighted I have been to have you as my guest."

The Countess had paused, then added:

"Perhaps it would be possible for me to invite you another time."

"Or perhaps you would have Thais," Anthea suggested tentatively.

"I might. Indeed, I might do that next year," the Countess replied.

Anthea knew that the invitations would be given if once again her God-mother needed an excuse to stay in London.

Anthea was sure that Thais, if she had the opportunity, would be far more successful than she had been in finding herself a husband.

But what did husbands matter when she had found a way to augment their income?

She would in the future be able to provide plenty of the luxuries they had been unable to afford.

"I have been so lucky!" she said aloud. "I have brought back clothes and discovered I have a talent that is really salable."

"You are clever, Anthea!" Chloe said in undisguised admiration.

Thais was more practical.

"How can you go on doing caricatures of people if you are not in London?" she asked.

"It will not be so easy," Anthea admitted, "except for the fact that I have made friends with the Marquess of Chale."

"A Marquess?" Chloe interposed. "Oh, Anthea, is he in love with you?"

"Not in the slightest!" Anthea laughed. "The Marquess is a very old man, over seventy, but he knows everybody and is the greatest gossip in the *Beau Monde*. I have asked him to write to me."

"Will he do so?" Thais asked.

It was a question that Anthea had already asked herself.

But she had discovered that the Marquess was an inveterate letter-writer and corresponded with his relatives and friends in the same prolific manner in which he talked.

"I am sure he will write to me," Anthea said confidently. "And if we search through magazines and newspapers, now that I know what the people look like, I am sure I can do sketches of them and make whatever they are doing appear funny."

"It is the most exciting thing that has ever happened!" Chloe exclaimed. "I wish we could tell Mama and Phebe but I suppose we will have to keep it to ourselves."

"We must indeed," Anthea answered, "and no-one must guess the real identity of Miss Ann Dale or . . . and listen to this, girls . . ." They turned their faces obediently towards hers as she said: ". . . or of the tiny little mouse that will appear in the corner of every one of my drawings."

"The country mouse!" Chloe exclaimed. "Did you really put it in?"

"It will be my trade-mark," Anthea answered. "I drew it to amuse you. Now I have decided that that will be my signature and, who knows, I may go down to posterity—just like James Gillray!"

"It is a thrilling idea," Chloe said, "but rather disappointing that nobody will ever know it is you. I cannot help thinking, Anthea, that by being anonymous you will miss half the fun."

"I shall also miss the recriminations," Anthea laughed, "and the brick-bats from those who think they have been insulted!"

"Will they really be angry?" Thais enquired.

Anthea shrugged her shoulders.

"I do not expect so," she replied. "The people in Society live in a world of their own. They think themselves too grand and too important for it to matter what the common people think!"

As she spoke she thought of the Duke.

She was quite sure he would not value anybody's opinion but his own.

He was, Anthea told herself, quite insufferably conceited and puffed up with his own importance!

At the same time, she could not help remembering that he was in fact the most handsome man she had seen during her visit to London.

Chapter Four

The Duke left his Phaeton with the groom and walked across the grass towards the Achilles statue.

At six o'clock in the morning the mists in Hyde Park were still insubstantial round the trunks of the trees and the grass was wet with dew.

There was a puzzled expression on the Duke's face as moving behind the statue he saw a veiled figure rise from a seat and utter a little cry.

"What in the name of God is all this about, Delphine?" he enquired as the Countess threw back her veil and raised an anguished face to his.

"I had to see you," she replied, "and it was the only way I could do so without Edward being aware of it."

"I thought I must be dreaming when I received your note an hour ago," the Duke said.

"Edward returned last night," the Countess said with a little quiver in her voice.

The Duke looked at her enquiringly and she went on:

"He had a very good reason for doing so. I have brought it with me."

She held out to the Duke what looked like a small scroll. He took it automatically before he said:

"Suppose we sit down? I see no point in being needlessly uncomfortable."

"Uncomfortable!" the Countess exclaimed. "Wait until you hear the reason why the Earl has come posting to London!"

She spoke in such an agitated manner that the Duke, after a quick glance at her face, seated himself on one of the Park-chairs which stood behind the statue and unrolled the scroll she had placed in his hand.

He saw immediately that it was a cartoon and remembered that the Earl of Sheldon had a collection of them.

As he looked at it in the pale morning light he saw that it depicted a very superior and autocratic-looking lion wearing a coronet and seated on a cushion which was emblazoned with his own coat-of-arms.

In front of him, clawing at him beseechingly, pleadingly, enticingly, were a number of small cats, all with the faces of very young girls.

But one of the lion's paws was placed protectively round a ginger-coloured cat with slanting but adoring green eyes, whose face undeniably resembled that of the Countess.

Beneath the cartoon was written simply:

THE LOVE OF THE PUSSYCATS

"Damnit!" the Duke ejaculated. "This is too much! Who the hell has done this?"

"I have no idea," the Countess said, "But you can imagine what Edward feels about it."

"It is not signed by either Rowlandson or Cruik-shank."

"Does it matter who drew it?" the Countess asked with a querulous note in her voice. "Edward is furious, as you can well imagine! For the first time he suspects that I have taken a lover, and I have had the greatest difficulty in convincing him otherwise."

"You have convinced him?" the Duke asked with a note of relief.

The Countess gave a deep sigh.

"Edward arrived at ten o'clock last night in a towering rage, swearing that he was considering divorcing me and citing you as corespondent!"

The Duke stiffened.

"I thought at first he would strike me, he was so incensed," the Countess went on. "Then he said that whether he divorced me or not he intended to close Sheldon House for good!

" 'You will stay in the country, where I can keep an eye on you,' he said. 'I have put up with your pre-

dilection for London and the raffish Society you prefer
for too long. In the future you will remain at the Castle,
and to make sure, we will reopen the Nurseries and
add to the numbers of our family.' "

The Countess gave a little sob.

"I could hardly believe it was Edward speaking to
me in such a manner, but he meant it, Garth. I swear
to you, he meant it!"

The Duke said nothing and after a moment the
Countess continued:

"You know how I loathe the country, and I am
too old to have any more children. Besides, without
being in London, without being able to go to parties
and meet amusing people, I swear if I did not die from
sheer *ennui* it would be because I had killed myself
first!"

"But His Lordship changed his mind?" the Duke
asked hopefully.

He realised that as usual the Countess was taking
a very long time to come to the point.

"It took me two hours to persuade him that he
was mistaken," the Countess answered. "Two hours
when I felt as if I were a martyr being tortured on the
rack."

"How did you persuade him?"

The Countess drew a deep breath.

"I told him that the cartoon was a sheer malicious
lie and that the reason we had been seen together so
much these past weeks is that you are engaged to be
married to my God-child, Anthea Forthingdale!"

"You told him what?"

The Duke's voice was as sharp as the report of a
pistol.

"I told Edward you were going to marry Anthea,
and, Garth, you will have to do so because otherwise
Edward swears he will not be convinced by my explanation."

"You must be crazy!" the Duke exclaimed. "I
have no intention of marrying a girl to whom I have
spoken hardly more than a half dozen words."

"You danced with her. You have seen her at the

parties I have given and those we have attended together."

"I saw her because she was staying in your house," the Duke said. "That does not say I have any wish to marry her."

"Of course you have no wish to marry her," the Countess agreed. "You love me, and I love you. But if you love me, Garth, you have to save us both from this terrible, ghastly situation."

The Duke said nothing. His lips were tight and his chin was very square.

He stared down at the cartoon.

"If you do not substantiate my story," the Countess said, "I am certain that Edward will go back to his original plan of divorcing me, and you can imagine what a scandal there will be."

"I do not believe he would do such a thing," the Duke said slowly.

"He would! You do not know Edward as I do," the Countess said. "His pride is hurt. There is no-one more proud than Edward and no-one more determined when he makes up his mind about something."

The Duke knew this was more or less true, but he said aloud:

"Perhaps I had better speak to the Earl."

"What could you say?" the Countess asked. "Except that the cartoon is a filthy libel. Do you suppose Edward will believe you?"

"Why not?" the Duke enquired.

"Because for one thing I am quite certain it is not only the cartoon which has upset him," the Countess replied, "but that someone has been talking."

The Duke did not speak and she continued:

"You know my mother-in-law, old though she is, has cronies who report to her everything I do. She always lets me know that she is *au fait* with my latest conquest."

She paused to say:

"And one can never trust servants."

"I thought you said you had a new staff."

"Not all of them," the Countess answered. "And

besides, I do not suppose they are above gossiping to the servants from the Castle, perhaps without even realising what harm they are doing."

That was, the Duke knew, something that could not be avoided, and too late he realised how indiscreet he had been to visit the Countess so frequently at Sheldon House in her husband's absence.

"There is only one thing to be done to save ourselves," the Countess said, "and that is for you to marry Anthea as quickly as possible."

"How can I do that?" the Duke asked impatiently. "And why the haste?"

"Because Edward has said that until you are married he absolutely forbids me to speak to you again, and I am to stay shut up in the Castle until Anthea is actually a Duchess.

" 'A broken engagement would be only too easy for Axminster,' he said. 'He can get out of his obligations, if in fact they have ever been made. You have made a fool of me for too long, Delphine, and this time I intend the laugh to be on your paramour—not on me!' "

"There must be a better way of coping with this," the Duke said slowly.

There was silence for a moment, then he said:

"I must of course ask you if you would prefer to come away with me."

The Countess looked at him in surprise.

"Do you mean that?"

"The only honourable thing I can do is to offer you my protection," he replied, "until such time as your husband can get a divorce passed through Parliament."

The Countess gave a little cry.

"Oh, Garth, it is adorable of you! But do you really imagine either of us could bear to live abroad, as the Herons had to do for years and years?"

She put her hand on the Duke's arm in a gesture of affection as she said:

"I shall never forget that you asked me, but the answer is—no. Definitely no, dearest Garth, because we would both hate every moment of our exile and would be clawing at each other's eyes within a month of reaching Paris."

The Duke took her hand in his and raised it to his lips.

"Whatever the penalties," he said, "I believe it would be preferable to what you are asking me to do."

"Nonsense!" the Countess said briskly. "Anthea is a very sweet girl. You have to marry sometime, and though the Forthingdales may be poor, their blood is ae blue as your own. She will make you a commendable Duchess, and you know as well as I do that you must have an heir."

There was no gainsaying this, but the Duke had never contemplated surrendering his freedom until it was absolutely necessary.

He had thought there was no need for him to think of marriage for at least another five years, or perhaps longer.

As if she read his thoughts, the Countess said softly:

"I am sorry, Garth, but there really is no alternative."

The Duke looked down at the cartoon as if he thought there might be some other way of repudiating its insinuation.

There was no denying that the expression on the lion's face, while a caricature, was unmistakably his own, or that the slanting green eyes of the ginger-coloured cat were all too obviously the Countess's.

It was a clever drawing and far more skilfully executed, he thought, than George Cruikshank's crude, vulgar style.

But its very delicacy made the cartoon all the more dangerous, and to be honest he well understood the Earl's anger at his wife being publicly pilloried.

"You will do it, Garth?" the Countess asked anxiously.

The Duke had been silent for some time.

"It is the only way you can save us both," she murmured.

"Then I suppose the answer is—yes," the Duke said grudgingly.

* * *

Anthea was in the kitchen rolling out the pastry for a chicken-pie she was making for dinner.

A large white apron covered her gown and because she had washed her hair the previous day, she had covered it with a protective white handkerchief.

All the girls could cook well, for their old Nurse had taught them when they were quite small.

When she retired to look after her sister who was ill, they had taken turns to prepare meals and often vied with one another in seeing who could produce the most delicious dishes.

As she worked, Anthea was thinking that now that she could make money, they would be able to afford Mrs. Harris from the village to come in two or three days a week to do the scrubbing.

That was the side of the housework they all disliked, and Thais always managed, if it was possible, to get out of her sahre.

Anthea was sure that her mother would be too vague to ask any awkward questions as to why Mrs. Harris was employed or how they could afford to pay her.

Anthea thought with satisfaction that waiting on the School-Room table were three more cartoons neatly packed up and waiting to be despatched to Mrs. Humphrey in London.

The main difficulty, she found, was to keep her drawings out of sight of her mother.

Rising early in the morning and working late after Lady Forthingdale had gone to bed was, she discovered, a better way than trying to hide what she was doing when her mother came unexpectedly into the School Room.

"Tell us about the pictures you have sold," Thais had asked.

"To tell you the truth," Anthea replied, "I have almost forgotten which they were. I drew them in my sketch-book whenever I had a moment, and I never anticipated when I showed them to Mrs. Humphrey that she would take the lot!"

She smiled.

"I just thought how lucky I would be if she bought one and gave me perhaps a pound for it so that I could buy you all a present."

"Ten pounds for each!" Chloe exclaimed. "It seems an unbelievable amount for those scrawls you have been doing ever since I can remember."

"You used to make us laugh with your drawings when we were children," Thais said. "It seems funny you should make the smart people in London laugh at them now."

"It seems funny to me too," Anthea agreed. "But I had better draw everything I can while it is all fresh in my mind. It would be mortifying if Mrs. Humphrey should return anything I sent her."

"I asked you to tell us about the ones you have sold," Thais said.

"There is no need for me to do that," Anthea said. "You will see them. Mrs. Humphrey has promised to send me one of each issue as soon as it is printed."

"You gave her this address?" Chloe asked.

"How could I help it?" Anthea asked. "But I can assure you that no-one in London is interested in Yorkshire except that some of the gentlemen occasionally attend the races at Doncaster, and elderly ladies take the waters at Harrogate."

"And of course no-one will have heard of Miss Ann Dale," Thais laughed.

"Or the Country Mouse," Chloe added.

"No, that is my safe-guard," Anthea had agreed.

She put the pastry over the pie-dish and cut the edge into an elegant pattern.

The girls all liked chicken-pie, and Anthea had found time to make one this afternoon, as everyone else was out.

Chloe and Phebe were having lessons and Thais had gone with Lady Forthingdale to Doncaster.

Once or twice a year an elderly Squire who lived

two miles away would drive into Doncaster for a meeting with the race-course officials.

When he did so he invariably invited Lady Forthingdale to accompany him.

As she seldom went out, her daughters always persuaded her that the drive would do her good.

"As a matter of fact," Lady Forthingdale had said yesterday when the Squire's invitation arrived, "I want to go to the Library in Doncaster. There is a book of poems by Lord Byron that I particularly wish to purchase."

"Lord Byron, Mama?" Anthea questioned. "Are you going romantic again?"

"I feel that His Lordship's work might be of assistance in the poem I have been considering this last week," Lady Forthingdale replied.

"I thought you would get back to love eventually!" Chloe said irrepressibly.

" 'Love is a malady without a cure,' " Anthea quoted with a smile.

"It is also 'a sickness full of woes,' " Thais interposed, who was as knowledgeable on her poets as Anthea was.

"I think you are making fun of me," Lady Forthingdale said with dignity. "But I do not wish any of you to laugh at love. It is something very beautiful which I hope one day will come into the lives of all of you."

"Nanny said once that it was unlucky to laugh at love," Phebe remarked.

"And so it is!" Lady Forthingdale said. "That reminds me, Anthea, I never asked if you had lost your heart to anyone while you were in London."

"No, Mama," Anthea replied. "I did not fall in love, simply because I met no-one as charming, handsome, or attractive as Papa."

She knew that her words would please her mother and Lady Forthingdale's eyes were suspiciously misty as she thought of the husband she had loved so dearly.

Irrepressibly the thought came to Anthea that, however handsome her father had been, the Duke undoubtedly would take the prize in a contest between them.

The pie was now ready to be put into the oven and she wondered as she opened the door of the ancient stove whether any of her God-mother's elegant friends were capable of cooking anything, even an egg.

The idea of their doing so in their elaborate gowns and glittering jewels made Anthea smile.

She was just wondering if that might give her an idea for a cartoon, when there came a loud knock on the front door.

She felt it might be the letter she was hoping for from the Marquess.

She had written to him on her return home to make quite certain that he would keep his promise to write to her.

Without bothering to remove her white apron, she ran from the kitchen through the Hall and pulled open the front door.

As she did so she gave a gasp of sheer astonishment.

Outside, there was an extremely elegant Phaeton pulled by four horses. Behind it were two out-riders in blue and gold livery, and behind them, just coming down the drive, was a Travelling-Chariot also pulled by four horses, escorted by two more out-riders.

As Anthea stared as if she could not believe her eyes, the servant who had knocked on the door said sharply:

"His Grace the Duke of Axminster calling on Lady Forthingdale. Is Her Ladyship at home?"

He spoke in the superior tone of a Senior servant addressing an underling.

While Anthea was finding it impossible to reply, the Duke stepped down from the Phaeton and came to the front door.

"Forgive my unexpected appearance, Miss Forthingdale," he said, "which I gather is a surprise."

"A . . . surprise?" Anthea repeated stupidly.

"It is obvious that you were not expecting me," the Duke said. "I wrote to your mother three days ago, but the posts are lamentably slow, and I imagine she could not have received my letter."

His eyes flickered over her apron as he spoke and Anthea realised how strange she must look.

"No . . . no," she faltered. "Mama has not . . . heard from you . . . and she is out this . . . afternoon."

"I still hope that I may have the pleasure of seeing her," the Duke said.

With an effort Anthea remembered her manners.

"Will you come in, Your Grace?"

"Thank you," the Duke said gravely.

He walked into the Hall. Anthea pulled the handkerchief from her head but was so bemused that she made no effort to take off her apron.

Instead, she led the way into the Drawing-Room and was relieved to see that it was quite tidy.

Three long windows opened on to the garden and there was a sweet fragrance from the freshly picked flowers in the big bowls which Anthea had arranged the previous day on various tables round the room.

"You are on your way to the Doncaster races, Your Grace?" she managed to say when they reached the hearth.

She indicated a comfortable chair on which the Duke could sit.

It was the only thing she could think of to explain why the Duke had called.

"In fact, I intend to stay the night with Lord Doncaster, who is a distant cousin," he replied, "but the races will not take place until next month."

"I had . . . forgotten."

There was a little silence. Then the Duke said:

"As your mother is not here, it would perhaps be best if I explained myself to you."

"Explained what?"

"The reason for my visit."

She looked at the Duke enquiringly, thinking that he must have a message from her God-mother.

After a moment's obvious hesitation the Duke said:

"In my letter, which should have arrived by now,

I asked your mother if she would permit me to pay my addresses to you!"

Anthea's eyes opened so wide that they seemed to fill her small face. Then after a moment she faltered:

"I do not . . . think I . . . understand."

"I am asking you to marry me, Miss Forthingdale!"

Again there was a silence that seemed to fill the whole room, before Anthea asked in a strange voice:

"Is this a . . . joke?"

"I assure you I am completely serious."

"B-but you . . . cannot . . . I mean, you . . . cannot . . ."

Anthea stopped stammering and said sharply:

"Why do you want to . . . marry me?"

"It is time I took a wife," the Duke answered baldly, "and I thought when we met in London that we seemed to be well suited."

Anthea rose to her feet.

"I cannot imagine, Your Grace, that you intended to be . . . insulting . . . but I cannot . . . credit for one moment that you expect me to . . . accept such an extraordinary and unexpected . . . suggestion."

"Why not?" the Duke asked. "I am usually considered extremely eligible."

"I am well . . . aware of that," Anthea answered, "but Your Grace is also aware that there are . . . reasons why I could not . . . contemplate such . . . a-an . . . i-idea."

She stammered over the last two words, feeling it impossible to express in words what she was thinking, and knowing quite well that he would not understand what was in her mind.

The Duke did not answer and after a moment Anthea said without looking at him:

"I think we have . . . nothing further to say to each . . . other . . . Your Grace, and as my mother will not be home for some hours . . . there is no point in your . . . waiting to see her."

As she spoke she had an urgent desire for the Duke to leave as quickly as possible.

She could not possibly imagine his motive for coming to ask her to marry him.

But she was certain that if he had spoken to her mother, it would be very difficult, without involving her God-mother, to explain why she could not accept him.

She had every intention of remaining loyal to the Countess, and she could only be thankful that she was alone in the house when he called.

Now, the sooner he departed, the less likelihood there would be of having to make difficult explanations of his presence.

"Please go," she said.

"I think I had best be frank with you, Miss Forthingdale," the Duke said.

"About what?" Anthea asked suspiciously.

"I had not intended to tell you the real reason why I am asking you to marry me," the Duke replied, "but perhaps it is the only way I can make you understand the urgency of it."

"I cannot imagine what you are talking about," Anthea said. "Let me make it quite clear that nothing Your Grace can say would make me agree to be your wife, and unless we mean to be involved in difficult explanations to my family, you should leave at once!"

Anthea glanced towards the clock on the mantelshelf as she spoke and saw with relief that it was only two o'clock.

That meant that unless anything unforeseen happened, it would be at least an hour before Chloe and Phebe returned from the village.

She could imagine only too well how curious they would be, to say the least of it, in fact astounded, by the Duke's entourage, which was waiting in the drive.

"I thought you seemed fond of your God-mother, Miss Forthingdale," the Duke said surprisingly.

"I am," Anthea answered.

"Then if you could save her from something very unpleasant, from a scandal which would completely ruin her life, would you not be prepared to do so?"

"Y-yes, of course," Anthea agreed, "but I . . ."

"The Earl of Sheldon is threatening either to divorce your God-mother, citing me as corespondent," the Duke said, "or to incarcerate her in the country and never permit her to visit London again!"

He spoke coldly and quite unemotionally.

"Oh, poor Cousin Delphine!" Anthea exclaimed. "Why should the Earl do that? What has happened?"

"I daresay you have seen those scurrilous caricatures of which the Earl has a notable collection," the Duke said.

Anthea was very still.

"The one that has caused all the trouble," he went on, "portrays your God-mother and me in a manner to which the Earl has taken great exception."

Anthea found it almost impossible to breath as he continued:

"The only way your God-mother could prevent His Lordship from putting his threats into action was to tell him that the reason I had been at Sheldon House so frequently during his absence was that you and I were engaged!"

"He . . . believed . . . that?"

Anthea's voice was so faint it was hardly audible.

"He agreed to accept such an explanation," the Duke replied, "on condition we were speedily married."

Anthea walked across the room to stand staring into the garden with unseeing eyes.

She could hardly believe that what she had heard was the truth.

She could hear the Marquess saying that a good laugh hurt nobody, and yet it was her cartoon which had precipitated this drama and caused the Duke to ask for her hand in marriage!

Her cartoon!

She had drawn it two days after the Duke had looked so bored when he danced with her at Almack's and after she had seen him enter the house later and thought he was a burglar!

She had disliked him and wanted to portray him at his most arrogant and autocratic!

She would not have cared if it hurt him, but she had never wished to hurt her God-mother or cause her a moment's unhappiness.

The Countess had been most kind and generous to her and she owed her a debt of gratitude.

Now the only way she could repay that debt was to marry the Duke!

'How can I . . . marry him? How . . . can I?' she asked herself.

Then she was sure that not only had the Duke spoken the truth but also that the Earl's threats were seriously intended.

She had not stayed for over a month at Sheldon House without realising that her God-mother was in fact considerably frightened of the Earl. The servants too spoke of him with an awe that invested him with an ominous presence, even when he was not there.

Although Anthea had heard a great many remarks about her God-mother, some of them disparaging, no-one had ever spoken of the Earl except with respect, sometimes grudgingly, but nevertheless respectfully.

"If you will do this for your God-mother," the Duke said from behind her, "I assure you that not only will she be extremely grateful, but so will I."

"But how . . . could we be . . . married in such ... circumstances?" Anthea asked.

"I see no difficulty about it," the Duke answered.

There was a challenging note in his voice.

Anthea realised without his putting it into words that anyone to whom he proposed marriage would be expected to accept eagerly and gratefully so distinguished a suitor.

It was only, she thought, because she had inadvertently learnt of the more intimate details of the Duke's love-life that she could not look on him the same way any other girl would.

It flashed through her mind that if in fact she had found in London the husband she was seeking, there would almost certainly be a skeleton in his cupboard of which she had no knowledge.

And yet she could remember all too vividly what she had felt when she saw the Duke going up to her God-mother's bed-room.

She could still hear the amused contempt in his

voice when he had told her not to interfere in other people's affairs!

At the same time, she had no-one except herself to thank for the predicament she was now in.

'How could I have been so foolish,' she asked herself frantically, 'as to include that particular cartoon with the others?'

She had in fact forgotten all about it.

'It was madness to have sold a cartoon which included Cousin Delphine,' she told herself now. 'Madness and at the same time unkind!'

Anthea had never been anything but kind; that was characteristic of her nature. She was always deeply touched by suffering or unhappiness.

She could be moved to tears by a tale of cruelty or privation.

She would listen with sympathy and patience to the grumbles and complaints of the villagers and would go to endless trouble to help them.

Yet without intending to, merely because she was bemused by the large sum of money which had been offered her, she had hurt the Countess.

'It was a malicious drawing in the first place,' she thought miserably. 'But it is too late now for recriminations.'

"I cannot believe that you are so heartless as to refuse to help your God-mother," the Duke remarked almost beguilingly.

Anthea found it impossible to reply and after a moment he said:

"Perhaps you are waiting for me to go down on one knee in the conventional fashion?"

Now there was a note of mockery in his voice and Anthea turned round to say sharply:

"There is no need for play-acting, Your Grace. You have been . . . frank with me, and I will be equally frank with . . . you. I have . . . no wish to . . . marry you, but in the . . . circumstances you make it . . . impossible for me to . . . refuse."

"I thought you would see sense," the Duke said, "and I assure you, Miss Forthingdale, I will do my best to make you happy."

"Thank . . . you."

As she spoke and her eyes met the Duke's, Anthea thought that they seemed to be challenging each other to a duel in which both were determined to be the victor.

"You will wish to be alone when you break the news to your mother," the Duke said after a moment. "So I hope she will be gracious enough to receive me tomorrow afternoon, when we can talk over the details of the wedding."

"That would be . . . best," Anthea conceded.

"Then I will continue on my journey," the Duke said, "but I would like to thank you in all sincerity for agreeing to my proposition."

Anthea inclined her head a little and he went on:

"I can assure you that your God-mother will be as grateful as I am. You have saved us both from something which would inevitably bring a lot of unhappiness and unpleasantness to a number of people."

Anthea knew he was speaking of his family.

She realised that he must have a great number of relations, all of whom she was certain would be absolutely astounded when they learnt who he was about to marry.

There seemed to be nothing more to say and for the first time Anthea was conscious of the white apron that covered her gown and that in their small house the Duke looked very large and overpowering.

As they were walking towards the Hall, the Duke noticed the portrait of Sir Walcott which stood over the mantelpiece.

"Is that your father?"

"Yes," Anthea replied.

"I see he was in the Scots Greys."

"Yes."

"I understand from your God-mother that he is dead. Was he perhaps killed at Waterloo?"

"Yes."

"I saw the charge," the Duke said. "It was magnificent! There has never been anything like it in the annals of British history."

"You were at Waterloo?"

"I was," the Duke replied. "We must talk about it sometime. I would like to learn more about your father."

Anthea knew he was trying to be pleasant but she felt as if she were frozen inside.

She pulled open the front door before he could reach it and drew a deep breath of fresh air.

The Duke's cavalcade and the livery of his servants made a vivid patch of colour and the whole entourage seemed even more incongruous than it had on its arrival.

It had nothing in common, Anthea thought, with the overgrown, unkept drive and the shabby exterior of the house, any more than she had anything in common with the tall, handsome, elegant man who stood beside her.

"I shall see you tomorrow," the Duke said.

She held out her hand and he raised it to his lips.

"Let me say once again how very grateful I am," he said in a low voice.

She did not answer.

He walked towards his Phaeton, swung himself up onto the high seat, took the reins from his groom, and turned his horses with an expertise which Anthea knew ranked him a Corinthian.

Then as he raised his high hat and his servants imitated him by raising theirs, the procession of carriages and horses swept back down the drive under the low branches of the oak trees and disappeared into the distance.

Anthea stood looking after them. Then she closed the door and put her hands up to her face.

It could not be true!

She must have dreamt the whole thing! How could she have known, how could she have guessed, that one cartoon, just one, should cause so much trouble and involve her in such a fantastic tangle?

Then as if galvanized by the horror of it, she ran to the School-Room to pick up the envelope lying on the table and tear it into a dozen small pieces.

"How could I have been so crazy, so naïve, so unimaginative?" she asked herself, "as to think that I could caricature the people I met and not expect repercussions?"

She could see now how mischievous her drawing had been, though she had done it merely to amuse her sisters.

As they had never seen her God-mother, she had known they would have no idea who the ginger-coloured cat might be.

It had merely amused her and balanced the picture to put the Countess in it.

When she had been sketching she had never for one moment expected the cartoons to be seen by anyone except Thais, Chloe, and Phebe. So she had exaggerated the characteristics of everyone she had drawn.

Now she was sure they must inevitably give offence.

There was one of Lord Alvanley, she remembered, with his cold apricot tarts and bed-side candles being extinguished under the bolster, which was very amusing. But he might not think so!

There was an even more provocative one of Colonel Dan McKinnon counting his locks of female hair and saying to his batman:

"I really must look round for an Albino, otherwise my collection is not complete!"

She had depicted him in the guise of a Sultan, with the concubines he had discarded and on whom he had turned his back weeping bitterly.

'I should not have done it,' Anthea thought. 'I should never have sold anything so intimate, so unkind.'

She wondered wildly whether she should rush to London to try to persuade Mrs. Humphrey to sell her back the cartoons which had not yet been published.

Then she told herself that while Mrs. Humphrey had seemed very pleasant, she was undoubtedly a business-woman.

Having sold her drawings outright, Anthea was quite certain that she would not now relinquish them, and she could only pray that none of the nine remaining cartoons would cause as much trouble as the first.

'No-one must ever know that I drew them,' she thought.

She felt herself trembling at the thought of how angry the Duke would be if he ever discovered that instead of being grateful to her he should in fact be cursing her for having involved them all in this frightening situation.

'The only thing I can do,' Anthea thought miserably, 'is to try to put things right by saving God-mama and the Duke from the Earl.'

At the same time, she thought, she would prefer to marry anyone . . . any man in the world . . . rather than the Duke.

She believed that he would, as he had promised, try to make her happy.

But how could she be happy, knowing that he not only loved her God-mother, but also that she had been instrumental in revealing their affection to the one person who should not have known of it—the Earl?

Anthea felt as if her head were whirling, and it was impossible to think clearly.

She only knew that the future seemed terrifying and full of quicksands.

"Supposing he ever discovers the truth?" she asked herself.

She was sure that if her God-mother was afraid of the Earl, she was likely to be far more frightened of the Duke.

'He is a very frightening person,' she thought.

She remembered his arrogance and unconcealed boredom when he had been forced to dance with her at Almack's.

"How can I bear a lifetime of that?" she asked.

As she did so she heard voices in the Hall, and knew that Chloe and Phebe had returned.

Chapter Five

Anthea stared at herself in the mirror and realised that she had never before looked so attractive—in fact almost beautiful.

She could indeed hardly believe it was her own reflection that she was seeing.

The exquisite and extremely elaborate wedding-gown which her God-mother had sent her from London was undoubtedly every woman's ideal gown for the most important moment in her life.

On her head Anthea wore a lace veil that had been in the Duke's family for generations, and surmounting it a diamond tiara fashioned in the shape of a wreath of flowers, which glittered and quivered with every movement she made.

"I did not believe anything could be so lovely!" Thais had said in an awed voice before she left for the Church with her mother and the other girls.

In fact the whole family, it seemed to Anthea, had been breathless with excitement ever since she had told them in an embarrassed manner that she was to marry the Duke.

After she had announced it on her mother's return from Doncaster, for a moment they had stared at her speechless.

Then there had been a babble of excitement which made it difficult for Anthea to make herself heard.

"The Duke of Axminster!" "But you hardly mentioned him in your letters!" "Why did you not tell us about him?" "How could you have been so secretive?"

The Duke's letter to Lady Forthingdale had in fact arrived the next day, but by that time the Duke had met Anthea's family.

She had expected them to hate him as she told herself she did, but to her astonishment he charmed them all.

"He is so handsome and exactly what a Duke should be!" Chloe cried.

Thais was beguiled into thinking him more romantic than any hero she had ever read about in a novel.

"He said such kind and complimentary things about Papa," Lady Forthingdale said later with a little throb in her voice, "and I know, Anthea, that he is just the husband Papa would have chosen for you had he been alive."

It was hard at times for Anthea not to cry out that she was acting a lie, that the Duke did not care for her; and that if she had a choice she would not marry him.

But because she felt so guilty and because she was so afraid he might discover her treachery, she forced herself to act the part which was expected of her.

The Duke had not only made himself extremely pleasant to her mother and to the girls, but he had also proved unexpectedly considerate.

Because he realised they had no servants, when he came to a meal he brought with him delicacies that required no cooking, and insisted that his servants should wait at table.

For the first time Thais, Chloe, and Phebe ate pâté de foie gras, boars's head, succulent hams, and game cooked in a manner which bore no resemblance to the plain boiling and roasting which had been the limit of Nanny's repertoire.

Exotic fruits from Lord Doncaster's greenhouses were also produced, and there were chocolates and bon-bons which were so expensive to buy that none of the girls had ever been given them before.

Besides all this the Duke, having discovered that his future mother-in-law was interested in poetry, brought her leather-bound volumes from the most expensive book-shop in Doncaster, which was a sure way to win her heart.

"He is bribing the family!" Anthea told herself scornfully, "just as my God-mother bribed me when she realised I knew her guilty secret!"

Although it made her try to disparage everything

the Duke brought with him to the house, she could not help realising that there was really no need for him to put himself out, as she had already agreed to do what he wished.

As it was, she found it hard to remain coldly aloof from the adulation which the Duke evoked in her sisters.

"He is wonderful! So kind, so understanding!" Thais would say.

"He remembers that I like sugared almonds," Phebe said. "I hope I find a husband as nice as him when I grow up."

It was Chloe, however, who was thrown into a state of stupefaction when the Duke said he would give her a horse to ride to hounds and would also provide and pay for a groom to look after it.

Overcome at achieving her greatest ambition, Chloe had thrown her arms round the Duke's neck and kissed him.

"Thank you! Thank you!" she cried. "It is the most wonderful thing that has ever happened to me!"

Anthea thought that the Duke for a moment stiffened with surprise at Chloe's demonstrativeness. Then he asked:

"If you are so grateful when you are given one hunter, what will you do when you receive a diamond necklace?"

"Who wants a necklace?" Chloe said scornfully. "I would much rather have a string of horses!"

The Duke laughed.

"I expect you will change your mind when you get older. All women like diamonds."

Because of what he had said to Chloe, Anthea had expected him to give her a diamond engagement-ring, doubtless one which already was part of the Axminster collection.

But instead he gave her a ring which showed that he had at least considered her as an individual.

After he and Anthea had announced their engagement and a notice of it had been sent to the *London Gazette,* the Duke returned to London.

Although she was glad to see him go, Anthea

found the curiosity of the neighbourhood hard to bear alone.

It was extraordinary, she thought cynically, how many people claimed her acquaintance now that she was to marry a Duke.

People she had no idea even existed called on Lady Forthingdale, and invitations to Balls and parties from every part of Yorkshire arrived every day.

"How kind people are!" Lady Forthingdale exclaimed.

"Kind?" Anthea replied. "They are not kind, Mama, they are only sucking up to us now because I am to marry a Duke! They paid no attention to us in the past."

"I expect they thought we were still in mourning for your dear father," Lady Forthingdale replied.

"You would make excuses for the devil himself, Mama!" Anthea said. "Personally, I would like to throw all their invitations in the fire and not bother to answer them!"

"I think that would be very rude, dearest, and even if you and His Grace do not wish to accept such hospitality, it would be nice for Thais, and later Chloe, to be included on their visiting lists."

"They will be included in the future," Anthea prophesied in a hard voice.

At the same time, it was difficult to be cynical when everyone was so anxious to be friendly and the wedding-presents began to arrive.

"Who are the Leightons, Mama?" Anthea asked as she opened a parcel containing a most magnificent pair of candelabra.

"I cannot recall their name for the moment," Lady Forthingdale replied. "Perhaps they are friends of the Duke's."

"The parcel is addressed to me and they live in Yorkshire."

"Then they must certainly be asked to the wedding," Lady Forthingdale said.

"It will be impossible to get any more into the Church," Anthea replied.

But even as she spoke she knew her mother would

invite the Leightons and there was nothing she could do to prevent it.

She had hoped that the Duke would not be in a hurry to be married.

But she thought, although he did not say so, that he was being urged by the Countess to get the ceremony over as soon as possible so that the Earl's suspicions could be finally laid to rest.

The wedding-day was arranged for the second week in July and the Countess wrote to Lady Forthingdale saying that she wished not only to give Anthea her wedding-gown and a most comprehensive trousseau, but also to provide bride's-maids' dresses for Thais, Chloe, and Phebe.

The girls were ecstatic with excitement and could talk of little else.

It was the Duke who brought the news of this act of generosity when he returned to Yorkshire for his second visit.

He arrived at the house late in the afternoon when the family were all together in the Drawing-Room and Lady Forthingdale was reciting to them a poem she had written in celebration of Anthea's marriage.

She had only just started the first line when there was a knock on the front door which, because it was so imperious, made Anthea know at once who had arrived.

"Who can that be?" Lady Forthingdale asked, arrested in the midst of her recitation.

"I will go and see," Chloe answered before anyone else could reply. "Wait until I come back, Mama, I do not want to miss a word."

She ran across the Hall and as Anthea had expected gave a cry of delight when she saw who was outside.

A moment later they heard her call out:

"It is the Duke! It is the Duke! He is back! Oh, is it not exciting?"

They had expected him shortly but had not been quite certain which day he would arrive.

Now as he walked into the Salon he seemed to

Anthea to be far too big and overpowering in the low-ceilinged room, and so elegantly and faultlessly dressed that he made even the furniture look shabby.

He raised Lady Forthingdale's hand to his lips, then turned towards Anthea.

She curtseyed but kept her eyes downcast, feeling that they might reveal that she was the only person present who was not pleased to see him.

Her coldness, if he realised it, did not perturb him.

Completely at his ease, he gave Lady Forthingdale the letter from the Countess in which she described the gifts she intended to make to all the family.

"How kind! How very kind!" Lady Forthingdale said as she read what her friend had written.

"I also have brought gifts," the Duke said, and obviously noted with a faint smile the light that appeared in Thais's, Chloe's, and Phebe's eyes.

"Sugared almonds!" Phebe said almost beneath her breath.

"Sugared almonds!" the Duke replied. "And other things as well!"

"Where are they?" Chloe asked.

"You will find them being unloaded in the Hall," he answered. "There is a very special present for your mother."

"Come and look! Oh, Mama, come and look!" Chloe cried.

Half-protesting and yet intrigued, Lady Forthingdale allowed herself to be swept out of the Sitting-Room and into the Hall.

The Duke and Anthea were left behind and although she had no wish to be alone with him she would not lower herself to run after her family.

"I have a present for you also, Anthea," he said.

"There is no need to give me one."

"I think everyone would consider it strange if I did not do so."

She realised then that he spoke of an engagement-ring, and because she thought she had been rude the colour rose in her cheeks.

He drew a jewel-box from his pocket and when he

opened it she saw not the diamonds she had expected
but instead a very beautiful ruby.

It was exquisitely set with diamonds and in its
depths glowed a mysterious fire.

"I thought rubies would become you," the Duke
said. "This is your own and not part of the family collection."

He took her left hand as he spoke and put the
ring on her third finger.

"Thank . . . you," Anthea managed to say, and
wondered why her fingers, because he touched them,
trembled a little.

"I hope it will make you happy," he said unexpectedly.

She longed to say that neither jewels nor gifts of
any sort could do that, since happiness must come
from the heart. But she was sure that he would not
understand.

Anyway, how could she make him happy when
she knew that he was yearning for the Countess and
that they were being married only to save her good
name?

Fortunately, there was no question of saying anything more because the girls, having collected the gifts
the Duke had brought for them from London, poured
back into the Drawing-Room.

They were wildly excited over a collection of new
books, a habit and a riding-whip for Chloe, a silk
shawl for Thais, and a whole number of small things
for Phebe which would keep her amused for months.

'I wonder who chose them for him?' Anthea
thought.

Then she told herself that doubtless he had well-
trained secretaries and servants who would be well
aware what sort of expensive presents he would be expected to give his fiancée and her family.

Then she remembered he had brought the Countess's letter with him!

So they had been seeing each other!

Perhaps now that their engagement was announced to the newspapers, the Earl was satisfied that
his suspicions were unfounded.

Or were they meeting clandestinely, prepared to risk discovery because they could not deny their love?

Anthea wondered what the Countess really felt about the Duke being married.

'If I were in love with a man,' she thought, 'I would hate him to marry someone else! I would be desperately jealous!'

Then she told herself she was being conceited in making herself of such importance. How could her beautiful, alluring, seductive God-mother be even remotely jealous of her?

The idea was ludicrous!

She was nothing but a country mouse!

But now, waiting to leave for the Church, Anthea had to admit to herself that the Duke had acted his part well, and that not even the most discerning onlooker would have suspected that their marriage was anything but a love-match.

Certainly not her mother or her sisters.

They were convinced that the Duke had fallen in love with her at first sight and she with him.

"Why did you not tell us about him?" Thais enquired over and over again.

Lady Forthingdale had the answer.

"When one is falling love, dearest," she said, "it is so magical, so ethereal, that one is almost afraid to breathe lest the wonder of it should disappear."

She smiled at Anthea.

"That is, I know, darling, something of what you felt, though it cannot be put adequately into words."

She gave a deep sigh.

"It is what I felt for your father, and I have always prayed that one day you would all feel the same."

"And that is how I would like to feel," Anthea said to her reflection in the mirror.

In two minutes' time she had to leave for the Church.

Downstairs, the Colonel of her father's Regiment had come to Yorkshire especially to give her away.

The little grey stone Church, which was only a short distance from the house, would be, she knew,

packed with not only their neighbours, but also relations and friends of the Duke's who were staying in all
the big houses in the vicinity.

Lord Doncaster had a house-party of thirty. Some
could find accommodation no nearer than York.

At first Anthea had felt shy and a little frightened
of the ordeal that awaited her. Then she told herself
that there was no point in feeling anything but coolly
practical.

This was a wedding where, instead of the bride
being on the threshold of a new and wonderful experience, she was merely a means to an end.

It was as if she had no identity of her own, but
was just serving as a life-line for the Duke and the
woman he loved.

"Yet how can I feel resentful," Anthea asked herself, "when it is entirely my own fault and I have
no-one to blame but myself?"

Mrs. Humphrey, as she had promised, had sent
her a copy of "The Love of the Pussycats" and
another cartoon which had been issued at the same
time.

When they arrived, Anthea had taken them to
the kitchen and burnt them in the stove.

She was always terrified that the girls would forget her instructions and make some reference to her
talent for drawing to the Duke.

But she had made them swear on everything they
considered holy that they would never speak of the
cartoons or the money she had made by selling them.

"He would never forgive me," she said, "if he had
the slightest idea that I had drawn anything so repre-
hensible."

"They might amuse him as they have amused
us," Thais suggested.

"He would be very shocked," Anthea replied,
"and unless you want him to go away and never speak
to any of us again, be very careful to keep my secret."

She knew this threat would be effective.

But to make quite certain there was no evidence
that could be used against her, she extracted the letters

she had written from London from her Mother's *sec-rétaire* and burnt those too.

Even the funny little sketches with which she had illustrated some of her letters could, if he saw them, give the Duke the idea that she might somehow be connected with the cartoon which had caused so much trouble!

The clock on the mantelpiece struck the hour and Anthea realised it was noon.

She must leave at once for the Church.

Because her home was far too small to accommodate so many guests, the Reception was to take place in Lord Doncaster's house.

It was nearly an hour's drive from the Church and the Duke had suggested that it would be best, as they had a long way to go south, if he and Anthea should leave after the ceremony.

"I cannot believe," he said, "that we will be greatly missed and I have no desire to make a speech or listen to one."

"No, of course not," Anthea agreed.

He had therefore arranged that they would return alone to the house for a light luncheon and for Anthea to change into her travelling-clothes.

Everyone else who was present at the Church would go on to Doncaster Hall, where there would be a six-foot-high wedding-cake and an enormous wedding-breakfast which would last late into the afternoon.

"How can you bear to miss all the fun?" Chloe had asked Anthea.

"I do not think I should enjoy it very much," she answered.

"Do not be so stupid," Thais said. "She wants to be alone with her husband, just as I would want to be."

She spoke with a quiver in her voice and a romantic look in her eyes and had no idea that her oldest sister gave a little shiver as she thought how frightened she was of being alone with the Duke.

'What shall I say to him?' she wondered frantically.

Then she told herself it was absolutely essential

that she should try to behave normally and not be in the least hysterical.

She remembered her father saying how much men disliked scenes.

"Women enjoy them!" Sir Walcott had said with a smile. "But I assure you that any normal man will run a mile rather than be involved in dramatics, hurt feelings, or tears."

"This would obviously come under the heading of 'dramatics,'" Anthea told herself, and she was determined to behave as her father would have wished.

She picked up her bouquet of roses and lilies-of-the-valley and turned to leave the bed-room.

As she did so the diamonds on her head glittered and the sunshine coming through the window seemed to envelope her like a blessing.

"I am acting a part in a play," Anthea said to herself, "and the only thing that matters is that I should prove a competent actress."

* * *

The Duke and Duchess of Axminster arrived at the Earl of Arksey's Mansion shortly after five o'clock.

Situated in a large Park, it was a notable example of Elizabethan architecture and looked extremely impressive as the four horses the Duke had been driving since they left home crossed the bridge over the lake.

"It is very large!" Anthea remarked.

"It has been added to over the years," the Duke replied. "But Arksey has redecorated a lot of the rooms recently and I think you will find it quite comfortable."

"I should imagine," she smiled, "it will certainly be more comfortable than a Posting-Inn, which would probably have been our alternative accommodation."

"I loathe Posting-Inns," the Duke remarked.

"I cannot imagine you have stayed in many of them," she replied. "When I travelled to London by Stage Coach I was horrified at what the average traveller encounters in such places."

"You travelled by Stage Coach?" the Duke asked in surprise.

"Unfortunately," Anthea replied, "we did not think that Dobbin would be able to complete the journey!"

The Duke, who had seen Dobbin, laughed.

"You keep forgetting that I am Cinderella," Anthea said, "or would you prefer to be King Cophetua while I am the Beggar Maid?"

"I think you resemble neither at the moment," the Duke said with a slightly dry note in his voice.

Anthea had to admit he was right.

The travelling coat of rose-pink satin which the Countess had sent her, with a high-brimmed bonnet trimmed with pink ostrich-feathers to match, made her look like a Princess in a fairy-story.

However, she found herself thinking again as she entered Arksey Hall that the whole thing was in fact more like a theatrical programme and everything she did and felt was pretence.

The great house formed the impressive backcloth, and when she found there were three maids to wait on her in the huge State Bed-Room in which, she was told, Queen Elizabeth had once slept, it was only another act of the play.

After a bath scented with rose-oil, Anthea put on a lovely gown of white gauze embroidered with silver, with silver ribbons and silver shoes to match.

As she walked down the broad staircase to the Salon, she almost expected to find an audience waiting to applaud her.

The Duke was waiting in the large room which overlooked the rose garden and had long windows opening on to a terrace.

He was standing with his back to her and as Anthea entered she thought how tall and commanding he was—a very fitting hero for the play in which she was envisaging herself.

She did not speak but he must have sensed her presence because he turned with a smile on his lips.

"You are very punctual," he said, "and may I say I appreciate that?"

"I have cooked too many meals myself not to be

sympathetic with the Chef who finds his soufflés falling
flat and his meat over-cooked," Anthea replied.

She walked towards the Duke as she spoke and
joined him to stand looking out at the garden.

"I love roses," she said. "And I am sure there is
nothing more beautiful than an English garden like this
one."

"Are you telling me," the Duke asked, "that you
would rather have stayed in England for our honeymoon?"

"No, of course not!" Anthea replied. "You know
how thrilled I am at the thought of visiting the battlefield of Waterloo, and it means so much to Mama."

"I am glad it pleases her," the Duke said lightly.
"At the same time, I want to show you not only where
your father died but also where I fought."

"I understand that you received the Waterloo
medal."

"I will show it to you when we are in London."

Anthea moved away from the window towards the
mantelshelf.

The Salon was very elegant. At the same time, it
was a trifle stiff, and she thought that they, too, were
being stiff and over-formal.

"I think I should tell you," the Duke said, "how
very becoming that gown is. What is more, it shows
off your rubies to perfection!"

Anthea put her hand up to her neck.

She had almost forgotten that a jewel-box had
been delivered early in the morning, containing a magnificent ruby necklace to match her ring.

"I am afraid I have not thanked you," she said.
"It was shamefully remiss of me, but there has been so
much to think about."

"Of course," he replied. "One does not get married very often!"

"Thank goodness for that!" Anthea exclaimed.
"Imagine if one had to have a commotion like this
every year, or even every five years."

"I think we will be quite content to wait for
twenty-five," the Duke said, "until our Silver Wedding."

'That is too long to contemplate,' Anthea thought in her heart, but aloud she said:

"I cannot imagine, after all the presents we have received, that we shall need any more silver. What will you do, as it is, with over fifty entrée dishes?"

"We might give a party."

"Or perhaps," Anthea said, "keep so many dogs that they can each eat out of a silver dish!"

The Duke laughed at the idea, but it flashed through Anthea's mind that she had sold a cartoon of the Duchess of York's one hundred dogs, with one complaining that he could not find his bowl!

Because she was embarrassed by her own thoughts, it was with relief that she heard the Butler announce that dinner was ready.

They went into the Dining-Room, where the Earl's Chef had surpassed himself by providing them with a meal that excelled any that Anthea had eaten in London.

There was champagne to drink and when the servants withdrew the Duke raised his glass.

"Your health, Anthea!" he said. "You have come through today with flying colours. I cannot think of anyone who would have carried off this somewhat difficult situation so magnificently!"

She was surprised at his praise and the note of sincerity in his voice. She felt the colour rising in her cheeks.

"Now you are embarrassing me!" she said. "I thought you behaved extremely commendably yourself, considering you were a reluctant bridegroom."

The Duke frowned as if he thought her remark tactless, but after a second's pause he said:

"I feel that we are starting out on a voyage of discovery. We really know very little about each other and we have seldom been alone together until now."

He smiled as he added:

"Your sisters, quite unintentionally, I am sure, are extremely effective Chaperons!"

"We have always done everything together," Anthea said. "In fact I feel tonight they will be depressed because they cannot be with me!"

"I think it would cause a great deal of comment," the Duke said in an amused voice, "if I set off for France not only with my bride but also with her three sisters!"

"They would have loved to see the battlefield," Anthea said a little wistfully.

"Perhaps we will take them another time," the Duke suggested.

Her eyes lit up.

"Do you mean that?"

Then she told herself that he was only speaking conventionally.

Once the formalities of their marriage were over he would be able to return to the Countess, and she would doubtless be left to amuse herself in the country, or anywhere else, provided that she did not intrude on his private life.

Because the idea was somewhat depressing she said quickly:

"Do you wish me to leave you while you drink your port?"

"I hope you will do nothing of the sort," the Duke answered. "I do not want any port, but I will tell the Butler to bring a decanter of brandy to the Salon."

Anthea rose to walk ahead of him down the long passage which led to the Hall.

As she did so she could see them both reflected in the gilt-framed mirrors on either side of the corridor.

The feeling of their enacting a play was intensified, and the Salon with its crystal chandeliers lit and the dusk falling outside the windows was very theatrical.

Because she had no idea what they should talk about, Anthea went round the room looking at the *objets d'art,* exclaiming in delight at snuff-boxes set with precious stones, at miniatures depicting the Earls of Arksey down the ages, and at exquisite pieces of Dresden china.

"I have a great many treasures at my houses in London and in the country," the Duke said, "which also I think will please you."

"Mama used to tell me how great noblemen possessed such beautiful things," Anthea said, "but it is always difficult to visualise them without actually seeing them."

"That is true," the Duke said, "and not only of seeing but of feeling."

"Yes, indeed," Anthea agreed. "One reads about people's emotions, of sorrow, of happiness, elation, ecstasy, and of course love, and one wonders what it would feel like to experience any of those one's self."

"Usually to be disappointed," the Duke said.

"Disappointed?" Anthea questioned.

"Particularly when it comes to love."

Anthea looked at him uncertainly.

"But surely," she said, "it is very wonderful and very exciting being in love?"

"It never quite reaches one's expectations," the Duke replied.

"Oh, but you must not say that!" Anthea exclaimed. "That means you are not really in love! Mama says that loving my father was far more marvellous, far more wonderful, than she ever dreamt it could be."

"Perhaps she was very lucky," the Duke remarked.

Anthea glanced at him a little uncertainly and wondered if he had quarrelled with the Countess or perhaps in some way she had failed him.

Because she had slept very little the night before and because she was so tired, Anthea suggested after they had talked a little while longer that she should go to bed.

"But of course," the Duke said. "And we have before us tomorrow another long stage of our journey south, so I am afraid you will have to rise early."

"Then I will certainly go to bed at once," Anthea said with a smile.

He escorted her into the Hall where there was a footman waiting to give her a candle in a silver candlestick.

Because the servant was present Anthea felt it

embarrassing to say good-night, so she merely smiled a little shyly at the Duke and walked up the staircase.

She thought as she did so how once again it seemed part of a play that maids should be waiting for her in her bed-room with candles alight on each side of the great, silk-canopied bed.

She put on one of the exquisite lace-embroidered nightgowns that her God-mother had sent her from London.

She slipped into bed as the maids extinguished all the candles except the two at the bed-side and as the door closed behind them Anthea lay back on the lace-edged pillows, looking round her.

Now she felt like the Princess in the fairy-story who was so blue-blooded and sensitive that she felt a pea under a dozen mattresses.

'It is all very exciting!' she thought. 'Exciting seeing this magnificent house, and very exciting to think of going abroad!'

She gave a little sigh which was almost one of happiness.

"There is nothing to be frightened of," she admonished herself. "The wedding has gone off smoothly, the Duke is good-tempered, in fact everybody is happy!"

She lay thinking of how pretty the girls had been in their pink gowns which made them look like rose-buds, and how her mother had shed tears of joy when she and the Duke had signed their names in the Vestry.

'In the future I will be able to look after the girls and Mama,' she thought.

The idea suddenly came to her that perhaps, after all, it was a good thing she had drawn the cartoon.

'If I had not done so I should be at home again skimping and saving,' she realised. 'Instead, Chloe has a horse to ride, I can give a Ball for Thais at Christmas —she need not wait until the Season—and Phebe can go to a really good school.'

She smiled as she turned over to blow out the candles by her bed and as she did so the door opened.

The Duke came into the room and Anthea looked at him in surprise.

He was wearing a long brocade robe of plum-coloured red which was becoming to his dark hair, and there was a touch of white at his neck which showed up the squareness of his jaw.

He walked towards her and only as he reached the bed did Anthea say:

"What is . . . it? Why are you . . . here?"

"You were not expecting me?" the Duke asked.

"Expecting you?" she asked in a puzzled voice, then added quickly: "You mean . . . you cannot mean . . ."

The Duke sat down on the side of the bed.

"I can see you are surprised, Anthea," he said, "but frankly I meant to talk to you before now about our marriage."

"What . . . about it?" Anthea asked nervously.

Her long dark hair was falling over her shoulders nearly to her waist, but the soft muslin of her night-gown was very transparent and did not disguise the whiteness of her neck or the soft curves of her breasts.

Her eyes were very large in her small face and there was an apprehensive look in them that had not been there before.

"We have been married in rather exceptional circumstances," the Duke said after a moment's pause, "but I think, Anthea, you will be sensible and wise enough to realise that it would be a very great mistake for our marriage to be anything but a normal one."

"What do you . . . mean by . . . normal?" Anthea asked a little above a whisper.

"I mean," the Duke said, "that we are man and wife, and that we should behave as an ordinary married couple would do."

"You . . . mean," Anthea said hesitatingly, "that you would . . . sleep here with me and make . . . m-make . . . love to me?"

"That is what would be expected, Anthea," the Duke said, "and that would be the right way to ensure that our marriage is successful."

"But . . . you could not . . . do that," Anthea said. "I could not . . . let you!"

"Why not?"

"Because . . ."

She found it difficult to go on and after a moment he said:

"You are thinking that my interests lie elsewhere. But, Anthea, you are old enough to realise that a wife has a very different position in a man's life from any other woman."

"B-but you are . . . in love with . . . someone else."

The Duke was silent for a moment, then he said:

"It may seem a difficult thing to ask, but surely you can forget what happened when you were in London?"

Anthea made a little gesture and he went on:

"You must have moved in the Social World long enough to realise that most men have liaisons of one sort or another before they marry. Usually their wives, especially if they are as young as you, do not hear of them, but—and perhaps it is a good thing—there is no need for any pretence between us."

"I . . . I married you," Anthea said, "because I knew it would . . . help my God-mother, but I never thought . . . I never dreamt that I should be expected to be your . . . real wife."

"I hoped you would not feel like that," the Duke said, "simply because it would make our relationship in the future extremely difficult, if not impossible, for both of us."

"If you . . . made love to me," Anthea said, "you would be . . . thinking of Cousin Delphine."

She thought the Duke stiffened before he said:

"I should be thinking of you and that you are my wife."

"I do not think that is possible," Anthea said. "How could you . . . kiss me and, even by . . . shutting your eyes, not be . . . thinking—'It should be Delphine! It should be Delphine'?"

She saw the Duke's lips tighten and thought he was angry, but for the moment she did not care.

"It would be just the same," she went on, "as when my Nanny used to give me nasty medicine as a child and say, 'If you hold your nose you will not taste it.' But it did not work!"

As if he could not help himself the Duke laughed.

"Really, Anthea, it is hardly a very apt simile!"

"I think it is very apt!" Anthea contradicted. "And I think it . . . wrong of you to . . . suggest what you . . . have!"

"I assumed you would be reasonable over this."

"It is not a question of being reasonable," Anthea answered. "You belong to Cousin Delphine. I have always thought it was wicked for someone to try to take away another woman's husband, and just as I would never do that, I would never try to take you away from the woman you love. You are hers . . . not mine."

The Duke rose to his feet to walk across the room to the fireplace, then he walked back again.

"I never envisaged for a moment that you would feel like this," he said.

"I do not know how you . . . expected me to feel!" Anthea said. "I think you are very handsome. . . . You are much nicer than I thought you would be. You have been very generous to the girls and to Mama . . . a-and . . . to me. But I do not . . . love you! How . . . could I?"

"Love is not entirely essential to marriage," the Duke said. "You are my wife, you bear my name. All I am suggesting is that we lead a normal married life."

"How can it be . . . normal," Anthea asked, "when if you make . . . love to me you would be . . . wishing you were . . . making love to Cousin Delphine?"

"Oh, my God!" the Duke ejaculated. "Is it not possible to make you understand what I am trying to say?"

Anthea did not answer and after a moment he came back to the bed to sit down on it and say:

"I do not want to sound exasperated or cross—I am not! It is just that I realise I am looking at it from a man's point of view, and you from a woman's."

"And because I am a . . . woman," Anthea said in

a very small voice, "I could not . . . let you . . . touch
me, when you . . . love someone else."

She sounded suddenly very weak and rather helpless and she added almost tearfully:

"I am . . . sorry. I am very . . . very sorry, when
you have been so . . . kind to us all, but I cannot do it
. . . I cannot really!"

She looked at the Duke and put out her hand.

"Please try to understand. I will do everything else
you want of me. I will look after you . . . I will obey
you . . . and because I know you would hate it I will
not make . . . scenes . . . never again after this one . . .
but please do not . . . do not . . . touch me!"

The Duke looked at her for a long moment and
because she could not help herself Anthea could not
look away from him.

Although she was appealing to him she felt somehow it was a battle of wills. She felt he was drawing
her, compelling her, forcing her!

Then when she was conscious that her heart was
beating and her mouth was dry, he capitulated.

"Very well, Anthea," he said. "It shall be as you
wish. I will sleep in my own room."

"Thank . . . you," Anthea said. "Thank you very
much . . . indeed . . . and please . . . try to . . . understand."

"I am trying," the Duke said.

Anthea gave a little sigh.

"As I have already said . . . you are much kinder
and nicer than I ever expected."

He rose to his feet and as he would have moved
away she said:

"You are not very . . . angry with . . . me?"

She put out her hand as she spoke. He took it
and raised it to his lips.

"Perhaps I am more disappointed than angry,"
he answered.

Then he went from the room, closing the door
behind him.

Chapter Six

Riding out from Brussels towards the battlefields of Waterloo, Anthea thought that she had never been so happy.

It seemed to her that every day she was with the Duke, it was easier to talk to him and everything became more exciting.

She had felt constrained and embarrassed the morning after their wedding-night. But she told herself that the worst thing she could do would be to erect a barrier between them which would make it impossible for her to talk to him naturally.

Everything was easy because she fancied, although she was not sure, that the Duke had speeded up their progress to the Continent.

Certainly they had stayed only one night at each of the important houses where they had been offered hospitality.

As they usually arrived late in the evening and left early in the morning and were therefore somewhat tired, there was not time to be bored by each other's conversation.

The weather was hot and sunny so the Duke drove his Phaeton.

The Travelling-Chariot either went ahead with the luggage so that everything was in readiness when they arrived, or was not far behind should they wish to ride in it.

Their cavalcade with four out-riders was very impressive and Anthea enjoyed the commotion they caused when they passed through small villages to be stared at open-mouthed by the yokels.

They passed one night at Axminster House in London and Anthea saw that it was in fact filled with the treasures of which the Duke had spoken, but she had little time to examine them.

By the time they had dined she was ready for bed, and they left early in the morning for the drive to Dover where they were to embark on the Duke's yacht.

Having never been at sea before, Anthea was apprehensive in case she should be sea-sick.

"Even though the Duke is not in love with me," she told herself, "I cannot imagine anything more undignified or unromantic."

But fortunately the sea was flat and there was only a breeze blowing in the right direction to carry them across the Channel.

Everything was so new and exciting to Anthea that her enthusiasm was irrepressible and the Duke found himself responding to her high spirits.

What was more, she made him laugh.

He could never remember spending a long time in the company of any woman unless he was enamoured of her and she was doing everything in her power to entice him and being very intense in the process.

Anthea, having made up her mind to be natural with the Duke, behaved as if he were one of her family or perhaps the brother she had never had.

She was wise enough to remember two things: first, that a man is always willing to give advice and to instruct; second, that just as she had been amused and entertained by the tales of the Marquess, so in the same way she could amuse the Duke.

Not of course with the tales of the *Beau Monde,* a world he knew better than she did, but of the life familiar to her, by which she had always managed to make her sisters laugh.

Because it came naturally to her she usually impersonated the people of whom she was talking: old Mrs. Ridgeway, the village beggar, the Vicar who frequently found Phebe's inquisitive questions embarrassing, the farmers who were always at odds with the rent-collectors, and a dozen other country characters.

She even included the loony boy who wandered round the village singing tuneless songs but was not so simple that he did not steal when he got the opportunity.

The Duke found himself amused by what Anthea was telling him, and he also found himself watching the sparkle in her eyes and the dimples in her cheeks.

Their honeymoon, although Anthea did not realise it, was a new experience for him as well as for her.

When they reached Brussels the Duke found that he had an attentive pupil who would listen with wide eyes to everything he told her and who never ceased asking pertinent and intelligent questions.

He had not brought his own horses with him, but he had sent a Courier ahead who had not only rented for them an impressive Mansion, but had also procured some fine blood-stock so that they could either drive or ride.

"It would be best for us to ride to the battle-field," the Duke had said this morning.

"I would prefer that," Anthea replied, "although I have not ridden a spirited horse for some time, so I hope I shall not disgrace myself."

"I will see you are on a mount that is not too frisky," the Duke promised.

When the horses were brought round Anthea was delighted with the chestnut mare which had been provided for her.

The Duke on the other hand was riding a head-strong, obstreperous stallion which was obviously in need of exercise.

He frisked about the road, shying at passers-by, but soon found that his rider intended to master him and there was no chance of his getting his own way.

Anthea knew that the Duke was enjoying the tussle, and there was in fact a look of satisfaction on his handsome face that was unmistakable.

The Countess had included in her trousseau an extremely attractive habit of deep red silk, almost the colour of her rubies, which was frogged with white braid matching the long gauze veil which encircled her high-crowned hat.

She looked exceedingly elegant, and although her face was a little serious as she concentrated on her riding as they moved through the town, the Duke knew she was enjoying herself.

He showed her the house in the Rue de la Blan-
chisserie which the Duke and Duchess of Richmond
had rented before the battle and where they had given
the Ball which had been immortalised by Lord
Byron's poem.

"Why did the Duchess of Richmond want to give
a Ball?" Anthea asked.

"The Duke of Wellington always believed that
psychologically it was wise to appear in public uncon-
cerned and for ordinary life to carry on as usual."

The Duke smiled.

"I was there when one day the Duchess of Richmond said to the Duke of Wellington:

" 'I do not wish to pry into your secrets, Duke,
but I wish to give a Ball, and all I ask is, may I give
my Ball?'

" 'Duchess,' the Duke replied, 'you may give your
Ball with the greatest safety, without fear of interrup-
tion!' "

"But he was wrong!" Anthea cried.

"Operations were not expected to begin before
the first of July."

"Tell me about the Ball. Was it very gay?"

Anthea smiled as she added:

"I know that 'The lamps shone o'er the fair wom-
en and brave men.' "

"The Ball-Room," the Duke replied, "had been
transformed with rich tent-like draperies and hangings
in the royal colours of crimson, gold, and black. The
pillars were wreathed in ribbons, leaves, and flowers."

"Oh, I wish I had seen it!" Anthea exclaimed.

"Byron's 'lamps,' " he went on, "were in fact the
most magnificent crystal chandeliers, and the 'brave
men' were headed by His Royal Highness the Prince
of Orange, and of course the Duke of Wellington himself."

"And you were with him?" Anthea questioned.

She already knew that the Duke had been on the
Duke of Wellington's staff.

"I was," the Duke replied. "And I was at his side
when the Duke learnt that some of the advance Prus-

sian forces had been repulsed by the French less than eight miles from Quatre Bras.

"The Prussians, under Marshal Blücher, were to join up with the British at Quatre Bras. Nepoleon had, however, begun his advance far sooner than was anticipated."

"How frightening!" Anthea said. "And what happened after that?"

"The news rapidly circulated round the Ball-Room that we were off the next morning," the Duke answered. "Most officers hastily said good-bye and departed. I waited for my Commander-in-Chief."

Anthea drew in her breath.

"Were you afraid?" she asked.

"Not in the slightest!" the Duke replied. "We were all extremely anxious to get to grips with the French."

They left the city behind and as they drew nearer to the battlefield Anthea was not surprised to see men and even women searching like beach-combers for souvenirs.

She had already learnt that there were stalls in the market-place offering for sale bullets, buttons, badges, and pieces of uniform.

And the Duke had told her that hundreds upon hundreds of English visitors had come to Belgium every month since the battle to wander about, sight-seeing and scavenging.

But Anthea was not interested in anything but the battle itself.

The Duke related how the three days had been wet and miserable with at times torrential rain.

"I remember," he went on, "how chilly the cross-roads to Quatre Bras were at six A.M. on June seventeenth, as we waited in a draughty hut made of branches for news of the battle."

The Duke's voice deepened as he said:

"It did not feel any warmer when we learnt Blücher's troops had been badly mauled just before nightfall, and had begun that morning to withdraw towards Warre, eighteen miles back."

Anthea could see that he was reliving the disappointment and apprehension they had all felt at the time.

"What happened?" she asked.

"We withdrew northwards about half-way towards Brussels. We had had practically no sleep, since fighting all the previous day to hold Quatre Bras!"

The Duke paused before he continued:

"We were all soaked to the skin. Many of the soldiers were so covered in mud that it was hard to recognise their uniforms."

Anthea and the Duke reached the ridge of Mont-Saint-Jean, where Wellington had made his headquarters in the village of Waterloo.

From there the Duke looked over the battlefield as if he were seeing it all happen again.

He could point out to her the Fort of Siogres on their left, and La Haye Sainte and Hougoumont ahead, both scenes of desperate fighting.

"The rain had poured down incessantly," he said, "and the ground became squelching mud. But if our Army was wet and miserable, so were the French!

"We learnt afterwards," he went on, "that Napoleon had said confidently, 'The Prussians and English cannot possibly link up for another two days!' He therefore decided to launch an assault on Wellington.

" 'The battle that is coming,' he told them, 'will save France and be celebrated in the annals of the world!' "

"When did the battle actually start?" Anthea asked.

"First there was desperate fighting for Hougoumont at about midday," the Duke replied, "and Wellington always said it was the gallantry of the Goldstreams there which saved the battle of Waterloo.

"Then the situation on the crest above La Haye Sainte became critical," he continued. "But many of us who had served in the Peninsula with Wellington were there. The Ninety-second were ordered to advance."

He gave a sigh.

"The Brigade had been reduced to fourteen hundred men by the fighting at Quatre Bras, but the Gordons, the Black Watch, and the Forty-fourth flung themselves with bayonets on the eight thousand Frenchmen —then . . ."

He paused dramatically.

"As the Gordons staggered under the weight of the massed French, they were aware of huge grey horses thundering down behind them with their riders uttering wild, exultant cries."

"It was the Scots Greys!" Anthea said hardly above a whisper.

"They swept through in a mad whirlwind of a charge such as had never before been launched by the British Cavalry."

Anthea felt her eyes fill with tears at the thought that her father had been amongst them.

"Behind them came the heavy Calvalry," the Duke went on. "As the bugle sounded the 'charge,' I heard someone shout: 'To Paris!' They went through like a torrent, shaking the very earth!"

Anthea shut her eyes.

She could visualise the Life Guards and the King's Dragoons wearing the classical helmets with horse-hair crests and plumes designed by the Prince Regent.

She could hear them thundering deep into the enemy lines until the French turned and fled!

Buglers sounded the rally, but no-one listened!

Two eagles were captured and fifteen guns in Napoleon's great battery disabled, while the French gunners sat on their limbers and wept.

"But they had charged too far," Anthea murmured, who had read the story of the Battle of Waterloo a thousand times.

"The whole valley behind them was flooded with French troops. They were cut off."

"And yet it was a victory."

"Despite the heavy casualties," the Duke said. "No Cavalry had ever before routed so great a body of Infantry in formation."

"It was the way Papa would have wished to die."

Then because Anthea did not want the Duke to see the tears which had suddenly begun to run down her cheeks she spurred her horse forward.

She was riding, she thought, over the same ground that her father had ridden in that wild charge when twenty-five hundred Cavalry had lost their lives.

The Duke rode after her and only came to her side when she had wiped away her tears.

"It was just here," he said quietly, "where we are now standing, that in the afternoon Wellington turned to one of his *Aides-de-Camp* and asked the time.

" 'Twenty minutes past four, Sir,'

" 'The battle is mine,' Wellington said, 'and if the Prussians arrive soon there will be an end to the war.' "

The Duke paused.

"As he spoke we heard the first Prussian guns."

"And that was the end?"

"Not for some hours yet," the Duke replied. "In fact not until eight P.M., and our Army was down to some thirty-five thousand men. The French were shaken, but not yet routed."

"Were you worried?" Anthea asked.

"Things had gone wrong. The Prussians had not yet been able to break through, and yet I think that everyone was supremely confident that the Duke could not fail."

"What happened?"

"At about seven-thirty P.M. the Duke was standing up in his stirrups at his Command Post by that tree. A ray of the setting sun threw into relief an unforgettable and indescribable expression on his face."

"What was happening?"

"We could see that the French extreme right was under cross-fire. Then someone cried: 'The Prussians have arrived!' "

"They had got through!" Anthea cried.

"This was the decisive moment," the Duke answered, "and every soldier knew it. I heard one of the Commanders advise limited action, but Wellington knew better.

" 'Oh, damnit!' he exclaimed. 'In for a penny— in for a pound!'

"He took off his hat and waved it three times towards the French. In a flash his signal was understood."

The Duke paused.

"Three deafening cheers of relief and exultation rang out as the Light Cavalry swooped onto the plain."

"And that was the end?" Anthea asked.

"Nothing could stop Wellington's men," the Duke replied. "Napoleon formed a reserve of his Old Guard into squares to stem the torrent, but it was impossible. Eventually he just had time to swing into his Berline and escape before he could be overtaken by the Prussians."

Anthea drew a deep breath.

The Duke had made it all seem so real.

"It was nine P.M. on Sunday the eighteenth of June and nearly dark when Marshal Blücher and Wellington rode forward to greet each other."

"Napoleon was finally defeated!"

"But at a terrible price!"

"Papa," Anthea whispered to herself.

"And fifteen thousand other British," the Duke said. "But the French had lost twenty-five thousand!"

"I hate war!" Anthea exclaimed.

"So did the Duke of Wellington. He said: 'I hope to God I have fought my last battle. It is a bad thing to be always fighting!' "

Anthea turned her horse towards the plain.

She felt as if the ghosts of those who had died there rode beside her.

Then something, perhaps it was the emotions surging within her, spurred her quiet horse from a trot to a gallop.

She felt the turf pounding beneath the mare's hoofs and she thought that she could understand the wild elation the Scots Greys had felt as they swept towards the French.

She remembered being told that in a charge the horses felt the same excitement as did their riders.

"Those terrible grey horses—how they fight!" Napoleon had said, watching from his mound.

Then she recalled how the Scots Greys had been cut off and that the Colonel was last seen with both his arms shot off and holding his bridle in his teeth. A friend of her father's, Captain Edward Kelly, had three horses shot under him. But he lived to survive the battle!

"My dearest, dear love," he wrote to his wife the next day, who showed the letter to Lady Forthingdale. "All my fine troopers knocked to pieces . . ."

A little shame-faced, Anthea pulled on her reins and checked her horse.

She looked back over her shoulder and realised in consternation that something had happened to the Duke.

She had thought he was following her, but now she saw that his horse was down on the ground and he himself was sprawled beside it.

Hastily she rode back.

As she reached him the stallion staggered to his feet and she saw that the animal must have caught his foot in a shell-hole and pitched the Duke over his head.

He was lying very still and she dismounted quickly.

Feeling that her horse was too quiet to wander far away, she left him free and crouched down at the Duke's side.

She turned him over onto his back and realised that he was unconscious. His eyes were closed and there was mud on his forehead. The skin was broken and she guessed that in the fall he must have struck his head on a stone which had knocked him out.

She suddenly felt desperately afraid and wondered frantically what she should do!

* * *

The Duke came slowly back to consciousness to realise he was lying on something soft and above his head he heard a voice say:

"Will you or will you not fetch help? I have promised you three louis, but I will make it five if you hurry."

Anthea was speaking in French and the man who answered her spoke in a rough *patois,* which was difficult to understand.

"I'll go, but I'll take one of the horses. It'll be quicker."

"You will do nothing of the sort!" Anthea said firmly. "How do I know that you will come back?"

"You'll have to trust me."

"I do not intend to trust you with a horse."

"What is to prevent me from taking one?"

"I will prevent you," Anthea said quietly.

The Duke felt her hand go into his pocket and draw forth the pistol that she knew he always carried when they were travelling.

She pointed it at the man and he spat at her:

"All right, Madame, but you're an Amazon —not a woman!"

"I would rather be an Amazon than a ghoulish sneak-thief from the corpses of dead men. Get on with you and be quick about it if you want your money."

The man must have gone, for the Duke heard Anthea give a little sigh of relief and realised he was lying in her lap.

"We will be—gone before he—returns," he managed to say with difficulty.

Anthea gave a cry.

"You are all right? I was so afraid when I found you that you might have broken your collarbone."

"I am—all right," the Duke said. "Give me a moment—or two—then we will—ride back."

"Do you think you can do that?" Anthea asked. "I imagine the man I was just talking to will wish to earn five louis."

"I shall be—surprised if he is any—help to us," the Duke muttered. "Assist me to my—feet."

It was not as easy as it sounded, because although he disliked having to admit it, he felt very dizzy. It took time and a great deal of effort before he could hoist himself onto the saddle of his horse.

Finally, with Anthea's help, he managed it and they moved at a very different pace back towards Brussels.

Afterwards Anthea often wondered how the Duke had managed to stay in the saddle.

She knew he was in pain and she learnt after the doctor had seen him that he had, as she suspected, a concussion.

"He will be all right, Madame, after two or three days in bed," the doctor said cheerfully. "But these big men fall heavily and he is lucky there are no bones broken."

They had been forced to ride home very slowly not only because the Duke was injured but also because the stallion was lame.

"It was my fault," Anthea told herself.

She realised it had been crazy to gallop over the battle-scarred field where there were deep holes made by the guns of the opposing Armies.

'I was fortunate,' she thought. 'But how could I have been so foolish as to involve the Duke for the second time in trouble?'

She felt chastened and rather depressed the first night when she had to dine alone.

Although she peeped into the Duke's bed-room to say good-night, he was asleep and could not speak to her.

Two days later he was better, if rather disagreeable, and to make amends for having been so stupid Anthea determined to be cheerful and not, as her father would have deprecated, to bore him with dramatics.

Instead, she amused him with some toys she had bought at the stalls in the market-place.

A toy monkey which had string to make him climb a pole, a puzzle fashioned from horse-nails on which the Duke spent a considerable time before he mastered the trick of it, and some funny little pictures of the battle showing Wellington with an enormous beak-nose to distinguish him from a moon-faced Napoleon.

"I have also brought you a special delicacy," Anthea said.

She sat down on the side of the Duke's bed and produced a cardboard box in which reposed the rich, succulent, and creamy *patisserie* for which the Belgians were famous.

"Do you feel like eating one?" she asked.

"I do not!" the Duke replied.

"Then as I could not bear to waste them," Anthea said, "I shall eat them myself! If they make me disgustingly fat I can always blame you!"

The Duke watched fascinated as she bit into a cake from which coffee cream oozed out between thin layers of sponge.

"How Phebe would enjoy this," Anthea said.

"I hope you are not suggesting that we take some back for her?" the Duke remarked.

Anthea considered the question for a moment.

"I suppose such delicate confections would not travel."

"I can assure you they would not!"

"It is a pity," Anthea said. "I think they are without exception the most delicious cakes I have ever tasted!"

The Duke shut his eyes as if the sight of them made him feel somewhat sick.

"I am not boring you, am I?" Anthea asked anxiously.

"Not in the least," he replied. "I intend to get up tomorrow. I am tired of staying in bed."

"No, no! You must not do that!" Anthea said hurriedly. "It is very important to rest when one has had a concussion; otherwise, as Nanny used to say, one becomes 'addle-pated'! Think what a disaster that would be for His Grace the Duke of Axminster!"

"I wonder if it would matter very much?" the Duke remarked.

"But of course it would matter!" Anthea said. "What will happen if you father a long time of half-witted Dukes?"

There was silence, and as Anthea realised what she had implied, the colour rose in her cheeks.

"It is of course a question," the Duke said, "of whether I shall produce a long line of any sort, intelligent or, as you say, addle-pated!"

Anthea jumped down from the bed and went to the window.

"Oh, look!" she exclaimed. "There is a man with a barrel-organ with a monkey on top of it. The sweetest little monkey, in a red coat. I wish the girls could see him!"

"It is a pity you cannot draw pictures of all you wish your sisters could see," the Duke remarked.

Anthea held her breath. Just for a moment the idea came to her that she might tell him the truth.

Supposing she told him? What would he say?

Then she knew it would be impossible. He would be furiously angry. And he would never forgive her!

They had in a strange sort of way, she thought, become friends on this journey; but that was not to say that he was not counting the days until he could return to the Countess.

They would have to be careful how they saw each other in the future, but the Earl presumably had believed her story now that the Duke was married.

"Once we get back to England," Anthea told herself, "the Duke will return to his own friends and his own interests. We will of course appear together on formal occasions, and perhaps he will want me to entertain for him occasionally, but otherwise . . ."

Her thoughts came to a full stop and she felt her spirits drop depressingly.

She was quite certain that the ease with which they now talked to each other, the way in which she could make him laugh, was only because they were alone on a conventional honeymoon from which it was impossible for him to escape.

"What are you thinking about, Anthea?"

She heard the Duke's voice from the bed and realised she had been silent for a long time.

"I . . . I was watching the monkey," she said quickly.

"And wishing your sisters were with you!" the Duke said.

Anthea did not reply and after a moment he said with a faint laugh:

"I must admit it is the first time in my life that I have been alone with a lady who was pining for the company of someone else!"

"Did I sound rude?" Anthea asked in consternation. "You know I have liked being with you. It has been very exciting and I have loved all that you have told me."

She looked at him anxiously as she went on:

"Although you are perhaps annoyed about what happened on the battlefield, to me it was a very moving experience to be there with . . . you."

She spoke very earnestly and for once she was not laughing or even smiling.

"I too have liked being with you, Anthea," the Duke said in his deep voice.

"Have you really?" Anthea asked. "You see, I have been very much afraid of boring you. You are so experienced. You have lived such a full life, while I have done nothing!"

"But you have thought and felt," the Duke said. "I realised when we were on the battlefield and you were thinking of your father that you were capable of deep feelings."

"I loved Papa," Anthea answered, "but I was not only thinking of him. I was thinking of those other men who died and how their wives, their mothers, and their sweethearts must have wept at their loss."

"As I have just said, you can feel, Anthea. That is very important. Most women do not feel very deeply about anything."

"Perhaps that is true of the women you know," Anthea replied. "But when Papa was killed, part of Mama died too. They loved each other so much. One had only to see them together to know what love is like."

"And that is what you hoped to find!" the Duke said.

Anthea looked away from him.

"I suppose . . . everyone has secret . . . dreams."

"And yours have been spoilt by me," the Duke said. "I am sorry, Anthea."

Anthea gave herself a little shake and suddenly her dimples reappeared.

"Can you imagine how your friends in the *Beau Monde* would laugh if they heard you?" she asked. "Apologising for marrying a Little Miss Nobody from Nowhere—a girl with no assets, who should be down on her knees thanking the gods of fortune for having sent her a real, live Duke!"

"If you talk to me like that, I swear I will spank you, Anthea!"

"You will have to catch me first," Anthea teased, "and that you will be unable to do until you have recovered from the wounds inflicted on you at the battlefield of Waterloo!"

She made a little grimace at him as she spoke.

Then before he could answer her she whisked out of the room, leaving him laughing rather weakly and trying to think of an answer to cap her repartee.

He was well aware that Anthea, with an ingenuity all her own, was entertaining him.

He knew that ordinarily, had he stayed in bed with nothing to do and a persistent head-ache, he would have loathed every moment of his enforced captivity.

But Anthea had contrived to keep him amused, and he found himself waiting impatiently for her to return to him and watching the door for her to appear.

His bruised head and the fact that at times it ached intolerably kept them in Brussels longer than the Duke had intended.

It was only because Anthea flatly refused to leave until the doctor permitted it that he was forced to bow to the medical dictum which made them stay an extra week.

Finally they left for England, their luggage considerably increased by the amount of presents that Anthea had bought for her family.

"Are you really very rich?" she had asked the Duke soon after he was laid up.

"I am not going to answer that question," he said, "until I know what it is you wish to buy."

The first purchase was an amusing peasant-costume which she knew would fit Phebe and which she would find fascinating.

The next day it was a gown for Thais, a riding hat for Chloe, and an exquisitely painted picture for her mother.

"What about yourself?" the Duke enquired after he had assured her he would not be bankrupt if she purchased all she wanted for her family.

"Me?" Anthea enquired, wide-eyed. "I want nothing. I have all these beautiful gowns. In fact so many of them that I think they will be out of fashion before you have seen them all!"

"They certainly become you," the Duke said. "You look very different from how you appeared that first night at Almack's."

"Do you remember that?" Anthea asked. "I shall never forget it. I hated you!"

"Hated me?" the Duke exclaimed in surprise.

"You did not want to dance with me, and when you did you looked so bored I thought you were insufferable!"

There was a note in her voice which told the Duke that he had hurt her and he put out his hand to say:

"I was obviously very remiss and exceedingly ill-mannered."

"It certainly made me hate you," Anthea said, "which was why . . ."

She bit back the words on her lips, knowing that quite inadvertently she had been about to say that this was why she had caricatured him.

He was watching her face.

"What were you going to say?"

"Which was why . . . I was glad you never asked me for another . . . dance."

But he knew that that was not the true answer.

Although the Duke swore he was completely well, Anthea had a feeling that when he was tired his headaches returned.

"You are not going to molly-coddle me any longer," he said. "You and my valets are nothing more than a lot of old women! You forget I was a soldier and used to hardships."

"You are getting older," Anthea said mischievously as she rose to leave him. "What you could put up with when you were a young man is not so easy when you are nearly middle-aged!"

They were talking alone in the Duke's bed-room. He had, with the doctor's permission, dressed, and was sitting in the window getting the fresh air.

He reached out and caught her wrist.

"I assure you I am well enough to give you the spanking you deserve! I have had quite enough of your sniping at me."

He pulled her towards him as he spoke and Anthea pretended to be frightened, striving to free herself as she cried:

"No, no! You must not over-tax your strength! Remember how weak you are!"

"I will not be called weak!" the Duke said grimly.

He caught hold of her other arm and held her in front of him so that it was impossible for her to escape.

"You are my prisoner! I have to decide now whether I shall beat you or kiss you!"

Laughing, her eyes met his and suddenly they were both very still.

Something passed between them, something magnetic and strange that Anthea had never known before, and yet it was unaccountably exciting.

It was difficult to breathe and her eyes seemed to fill her small face.

Then the Duke released her.

"I think it is . . . time for your . . . tea," Anthea murmured incoherently and fled from the room.

They left Brussels two days later and reached London without mishap, having stayed the night at Canterbury rather than do the journey from Dover in one day, as they had done on the outward journey.

They therefore arrived at Axminster House at four o'clock the following afternoon.

"Welcome home, Your Grace," the Butler said to Anthea as she stepped into the huge marble Hall.

"Is everything all right, Dorkins?" the Duke enquired.

"Everything, Your Grace. There's tea in the Library, and wine, if Your Grace prefers."

"I think you should have a little wine," Anthea said before the Duke could speak. "I am sure you are feeling tired."

"I am feeling nothing of the sort!" the Duke said firmly, conscious of a head-ache which he had determined not to acknowledge.

Anthea glanced at him in a way which told him that she was not deceived, then walked ahead of him.

The Library, which looked on to the garden, was at the back of the house. She had learnt that the Duke habitually sat there.

Although it was called the Library, it was in fact a very large and very beautiful Sitting-Room and in Anthea's mind far more comfortable and less formal than the big Salons on the first floor.

There was a tea-table glittering with silver drawn up beside an arm-chair, and on it every type of delicacy to tempt their appetites—sandwiches, scones, and a number of different sorts of cake.

"Can you really be hungry?" the Duke asked in an amused voice as Dorkins poured him out a glass of champagne.

"It is tea-time," Anthea replied a little reproachfully. "At home we always have Nursery tea with hot buttered toast and crumpets in the winter, and cucumber sandwiches in the summer."

"I have a feeling you ate a large number while you were preparing them!" the Duke said.

"That is why I am hungry now," Anthea smiled.

"If there is anything else you require, Your Grace, if you will just touch the bell," Dorkins murmured.

"I am sure we have everything!" Anthea answered.

"A great number of letters have arrived for Your Graces," the Butler said. "I have placed them on the table with the presents which came after you left. Some of them have been sent on from Yorkshire."

Anthea jumped to her feet.

"Yorkshire!" she exclaimed. "Then of course there should be a letter from home!"

She hurried across the room without waiting for Dorkins to bring the letters to her and found, as she had expected, one in her mother's hand-writing and one in Thais's.

"How exciting!" she cried. "We shall know now whether they received the letters I sent to them!"

She took the letters in her hand and returned to sit at the tea-table.

The Duke, who had followed her across the room, stood looking at the pile of presents.

They had been opened by his secretary but were arranged neatly with the card of the sender tied onto each one.

"More entrée dishes!" he groaned.

"Just listen to what Thais says," Anthea cried. "She is very funny about the Reception and she says that without us it was like *Hamlet* without the Prince! Phebe ate six pieces of wedding-cake and felt sick all the way home.

"Oh, and listen to this . . ." she continued.

"Everyone said You were the most beautiful Couple they had ever seen. The Duke was so handsome that Chloe swears She saw several Women almost fainting when He walked down the Aisle, and You looked lovely, Dearest, you did really!

We were all so proud of You. Come back soon! We long to see You and We want to hear all about Your Honeymoon.

Mama says that that is when two People visit 'the blessed Isles of Bliss.'

All our love,

Your affectionate sister,

Thais

P.S. . . ."

Anthea was just about to read the postscript aloud when she stopped. She saw that Thais had written:

A lot more of Your Cartoons arrived, and as I thought You would like to see Them I have put them in the same Box as a quite nauseatingly ugly Garnet Necklace which has been sent to You by a Cousin that no-one has ever heard of! They are very funny, Anthea, and made Chloe and me laugh a lot!

Hastily Anthea folded the letter and put it into the pocket of her travelling-gown.

For the first time she realised that the wedding-presents had been unpacked, and feeling suddenly afraid, she walked quickly across the Library to where the Duke was standing.

As she reached him he held out a letter he had been reading and said in a voice she hardly recognised:

"Perhaps you would like to explain this?"

Anthea saw the heading on the writing-paper and felt as if she were turned to stone.

Automatically, hardly knowing what she did, she took it from him and the words seemed to flash in front of her eyes like a streak of lightning.

Dear Miss Dale:

I enclose Copies of the other eight of your Cartoons which we have published all together as there has been such a demand for the first Two.

I know You will be interested to hear that "The Love of the Pussycats" has now sold over Three Hundred Copies! Please let Us have some more of your Work as soon as possible.

I remain,
Yours respectfully,
Hannah Humphrey.

Anthea looked up at the Duke, saw the expression on his face, and gave a little cry.

Clutching the letter tightly in her hand, she turned and ran from the room in a panic, frightened as she had never been frightened before.

Chapter Seven

Anthea came out the back door of the cottage and threw a basin of water over the marigolds.

When she had done so, two cats followed her back into the house to sit watching her with unblinking green eyes as she stirred a saucepan on the ancient stove.

"Dinner is not ready yet," she said to them, "so you will have to wait."

She found it comforting to talk to the cats.

Having always lived in a family, she found the silence and the loneliness of Elderberry Cottage at times so oppressive that she felt she could bear it no longer.

And yet, she asked herself, what else could she do?

She had run away from Axminster House because she could not face the Duke.

Afterwards, she wondered how it could have been so easy. She had not had to think or plan but had acted merely on impulse.

She had rushed from the Library upstairs to her bed-room and found there were three housemaids unpacking her trunks.

She saw that her travelling-cape and bonnet were laid on a chair. Beside them she noticed a valise which during their travels had contained most of what she required for one night.

Without considering, hardly realising what she was doing, Anthea put on her bonnet and cape and said to one of the maids:

"Carry this valise downstairs for me."

She had gone ahead down the Grand Staircase to find there was only one footman on duty in the Hall.

"I require a hackney-carriage."

The flunkey looked surprised but hurried out obediently into the street to find one.

Two minutes later Anthea was driving away from Axminster House and the Duke.

She had told the coachman to drive to The Lamb at Islington, meaning to take a Stage Coach home. But as she drove there she had thought that Yorkshire was the first place the Duke would look for her.

She was afraid not only of his anger but also of her mother's distress.

Anthea realised only too well how horrified Lady Forthingdale would be that she had lampooned her God-mother and precipitated such a disastrous sequence of events.

It would be impossible to keep from her the knowledge that the Duke had proposed not out of affection but merely to save himself and the woman he loved from being implicated in a divorce.

"Mama would be shocked and miserable!" Anthea told herself.

By the time the hackney-carriage had arrived at Islington she had made up her mind.

She would not go back to Yorkshire. Instead, she would go and stay with her old Nurse.

No-one would suspect that she was there, and in weeks, or perhaps months, everything would have calmed down and she herself would be able to face the music.

It was not going to be easy, Anthea was aware of that.

The thought of the Duke's anger made her tremble, but it was not only his anger she feared.

As she journeyed towards Cumberton in Worcestershire where her Nurse lived, she began to face the truth.

She was indeed afraid of what the Duke might say to her, but most of all she regretted losing his friendship.

'I liked being with him. I enjoyed listening to him talking to me. It was wonderful when I made him laugh,' she thought.

Then even as she half put into words what she felt, she knew it was not just friendship she had for him but something far deeper and far more disturbing.

"I love . . . him! I love . . . him!" she finally admitted to herself when she stayed the night at a Posting-Inn and was allotted a small, hard bed in the attic.

It was very different from the luxury she had enjoyed on her honeymoon.

That had all been so comfortable and extravagant and unlike anything she had known before, but she knew now it was not the material comforts which had mattered.

Everything had seemed gay and exciting simply because the Duke was there.

"How blind of me not to realise it before!" she told herself.

She wondered how she could have failed to understand her feelings when her heart had leapt whenever she saw him; how it had been an enchantment to drive beside him and to hear his deep voice explaining so many things which she wanted to know.

"He understood what I felt about Papa on the battlefield," she had told herself.

She had tried to hide her tears, but he had seen them.

"You can feel, Anthea," he had said, "That is very important. Most women do not feel very deeply about anything."

"What did he mean," Anthea asked now, "by saying it was important? Important to whom?"

She knew the answer to that.

He was in love with Cousin Delphine and although he might have found his honeymoon less tedious than he had anticipated, she was nothing in his life except the wife he did not want.

"I . . . love him! Oh, God, I love . . . him!" Anthea cried despairingly into the darkness.

The misery she was feeling was worse than anything she had experienced before in her life.

It was an agony and a despair which made her
wish that she had never gone to London and never met
the Duke.

How could she have guessed that love would be
like this?

It was not the blissful emotion of which her mother had talked, but something agonizing which tortured
her because she knew her love could never be requited
and that because of it she would never laugh again.

She wished now that she had let the Duke make
her truly his wife as he had wanted to do.

If he had kissed her, if he had held her in his
arms, whoever he might have been thinking of, it
would have been better than to know that she would
have no memories of love in the empty years that lay
ahead.

"If only he had . . . kissed me . . . just once," her
heart cried.

* * *

It took Anthea the whole of the next day to reach
Pershore in Worcestershire, and from there she found
a carrier's-cart to take her to Cumberton.

It was a small village, just as her Nurse had often
described it to her, with a dozen black-and-white
thatched cottages standing round a village green.

There was an ancient Inn called The Pelican
and a duck-pond in which witches had endured trial
by water in mediaeval times.

The carrier, who was conveying some barrels of
ale to The Pelican, set her down, and Anthea, seeing a
small boy eyeing her with curiosity, asked him the
way to Elderberry Cottage.

"It be at th'end o'th'village," he answered.

"Will you carry my valise for me?" Anthea asked.
"I will give you two pence if you will do so."

The boy, whose name she learnt was Billy, was
only too willing to oblige and they set off side by side.

Anthea was aware that several faces had appeared
at the cottage windows, obviously surprised not only

at her smart appearance but also at the arrival of a stranger.

"I expect you know Miss Tuckett," Anthea said to Billy.

"Aye, Oi knows 'er all right, but 'er be dead!"

"Surely not?" Anthea exclaimed. "You must mean her sister, Mrs. Cosnet, who I knew was ill."

"They both be dead," Billy insisted. "Missie Tuckett, 'er be buried two weeks ago cum Thursday."

"I cannot believe it!" Anthea exclaimed in consternation.

She had known that Nanny's widowed sister was very ill when she had left Yorkshire to nurse her, but she had written several times to say she was better in health.

Nanny had written to congratulate her on her approaching marriage and she had written back to thank her and say how much she wished she could be at the ceremony.

But dead!

When she fled from London she had thought, child-like, that Nanny would always be there to look after her.

It was an unhappiness she could hardly bear, to know that Nanny was dead and she would never see her again.

"What am I to do?" she asked helplessly of the small boy beside her.

"Mrs. Weldon, 'er who lives next door, 'as th'key," he volunteered.

"Then I will go to the cottage," Anthea decided.

She was to learn in the next few days that the whole village had in fact been expecting her to arrive.

"Your Nurse, and a wonderful woman she was, wrote a letter to you," the Vicar said, "saying that she was ill and telling you that if anything should happen to her the cottage and its contents were to be yours and your sisters'."

He paused to add:

"She was a little rambling, but I think I am right

in saying that you are Miss Anthea and your sisters are Thais, Chloe, and Phebe?"

"You are quite right!" Anthea answered.

She realised as the Vicar went on talking that Nanny had not mentioned the fact that she was to be married and he had no idea that she was not still Miss Forthingdale.

She was relieved that she did not have to tell him her real name and surreptitiously, when he was not looking, she removed her wedding-ring.

"I am quite certain you would not wish to settle in Cumberton, Miss Forthingdale," the Vicar was saying, "but it is a nice little cottage and, if you should wish to sell it, I am quite certain I can find a purchaser."

"Thank you, Vicar," Anthea said, "but for the moment I will stay and tidy up Nanny's things."

"That is right, Miss Forthingdale, do nothing in a hurry," the Vicar smiled. "It is always wise to sleep on a decision, whatever it may be."

Anthea found, however, that there was little to tidy.

Nanny had always been meticulously particular when she lived with them and her house was "as clean as a new pin," as she herself would have said.

Mrs. Weldon had looked after Nanny's two cats, which as soon as they found that Anthea was staying at Elderberry Cottage returned to their home, demanding food at least twice a day.

This meant that Anthea had to cook, however depressed she might feel.

She often thought that if she had been alone she would just have sat and moped and made no effort to feed herself.

But Antony and Cleopatra, as she had named the cats, were very sure what they required and had no compunction about complaining noisily if their meals were overdue.

She stirred the pot now in which a large rabbit was cooking and thought they were more importunate than any husband might be.

Even to think of the Duke was to feel a sharp stab of unhappiness within her, and she wondered if she would ever be free of the heavy weight of misery that was like a stone within her breast.

She wondered if he missed her, or if in fact he had been glad to be rid of her.

He would suppose she had gone back to Yorkshire, and this would have relieved him of feeling any embarrassment about being with the Countess again.

Cleopatra's green eyes reminded her of Cousin Delphine's and she thought again and again, as she looked at the cat, of the mischief-making cartoon that had caused all the trouble.

"How could I have done it?" she asked herself for the thousandth time.

She heard again the sharp note in the Duke's voice as he had handed her Mrs. Humphrey's letter and asked:

"Perhaps you would like to explain this?"

How could she explain it? How could she explain anything except that he would never forgive her?

A tear dropped onto the stove and made a little sizzling sound.

Fiercely Anthea wiped her eyes with the back of her hand. What was the point of crying? It only gave her a head-ache.

There was a knock at the door and she thought it must be Billy bringing her some purchases from the small shop at the other end of the village.

She turned from the stove, walked towards the door, and opened it to stand transfixed.

It was not Billy who stood there, but the Duke!

She looked at him with a stricken expression.

"Good-evening, Anthea!"

It was impossible for Anthea to find her voice.

She could only stare at him, thinking he looked even more handsome, larger, and more overpowering than when she had last seen him.

"I would like to come in!" the Duke said after a long silence. "But I am not quite certain what to do about Hercules."

Anthea looked with bemused eyes to see a black stallion tethered by his bridle to a wooden paling next to the gate.

She opened her lips to speak but no sound came, and at that moment Billy appeared.

"That be a fine 'orse, Missie!" he said appreciatively.

"Will you . . . lead him to . . . Mr. Clements and ask him to put . . . the horse . . . in his stables, rub him down, and . . . feed him?" Anthea asked in a voice that sounded strange even to herself.

"That Oi will, Missie," Billy said with relish. "'Ere's th' things ye wanted."

He thrust a package into Anthea's hand and lifting the bridle from the fence started to lead the horse down the road.

"Clements was a . . . groom before he . . . retired," Anthea explained to the Duke. "Your horse will be quite . . . safe with . . . him."

She walked back into the cottage to put the package which Billy had brought her down on the table.

"I can see you are very cozy here," the Duke said. "I am sure your Nurse is looking after you well."

"Nanny is . . . dead!"

There was a throb in her voice. It was difficult to speak of it.

"I am sorry about that. Then you are here alone?"

"Y-yes."

She glanced towards him and looked away again. She had not realised before how very small the cottage was.

He seemed too big for the tiny room and his head almost touched the oak beams crossing the ceiling.

"I have ridden a long way," the Duke said. "I wonder if I could have a drink?"

"Of course," Anthea replied. "I have some cider, or when Billy returns he can fetch you something from the Inn."

"Cider will do well."

The Duke sat down on a hard chair beside the

table as Anthea brought a bottle from a cupboard and put a tumbler down in front of him.

She then went back to the stove to stir the rabbit in the pot, her back to the Duke.

He watched her as he drank the cider. Then he said:

"I have also had nothing to eat since noon and then it was not a very substantial meal."

"I have nothing to offer you but rabbit," Anthea said, "and that is really for the cats."

"I have a feeling they are already over-fed," the Duke said, "while you are looking very thin, Anthea."

"I . . . have not been . . . hungry."

The Duke glanced at Cleopatra and Antony, who eyed him balefully.

"I am very fond of rabbit!" he said firmly.

Anthea brought a clean linen cloth from a drawer and laid it over the table.

Then she set a knife and fork in front of the Duke and put a plate near the stove to warm.

"I have a dislike of eating alone," the Duke said, "and although I have a feeling your cats will accept an invitation with alacrity, I would rather you joined me, Anthea."

She put another plate to warm and laid another knife and fork without looking at him. She also put a cottage loaf of fresh bread and a pat of butter on the table.

"That looks extremely good!" the Duke said.

"There are a few strawberries and a small cream-cheese, otherwise the larder is empty."

"I am too hungry to be particular," the Duke answered. "I am looking forward to the rabbit."

There were no vegetables, so Anthea went into the garden and cut a lettuce. She also found several tomatoes which had ripened in the sun.

She thought as she went back into the cottage that the Duke looked very much at his ease. But his riding-boots were dusty and she knew that he must have ridden hard.

"How did you . . . find me?" she managed to ask as he cut himself a large crust from the cottage loaf.

"Thais told me."

Anthea started.

"Thais? You have . . . been to . . . Yorkshire?"

"I thought you would have gone home," he replied, "but when I realised you were not there I was very tactful."

"You did . . . not tell . . . Mama?"

"No, of course not," he answered, "and when I realised that none of them had heard from you I took Thais on one side and told her the truth."

Anthea was unable to meet his eyes.

The thought of the Duke and Thais discussing the cartoons she had drawn made her feel more humiliated than she had before.

"It was Thais," the Duke went on, "who guessed that you would come here, so you can realise that I have done a lot of travelling in the last week."

Anthea started.

"Your head!" she exclaimed. "You have not had your head-aches again?"

"Occasionally," the Duke admitted, "but it was only because I was doing more than perhaps was expedient."

"I . . . I am . . . sorry."

She told herself this was one more thing she had done wrong, one more way in which she had damaged the Duke.

She was quite certain he should never have undertaken such an arduous journey as going all the way to Yorkshire and then down to Worcestershire so soon after he had returned from the Continent.

The rabbit was ready and having tipped it from the sauce-pan into a china dish, she brought it to the table.

She remembered there was vinegar in the cupboard for the salad and also a pot of home-made red-currant jelly.

Nanny would never let a season go by without making the fruit into jams, and Anthea had not forgotten that ever since she was a child she had always found them delicious.

"I suppose it is because I am very hungry," the

Duke said, "but I do not think I have ever tasted a more delectable rabbit!"

Because she thought it would please him, Anthea put a little on her own plate.

Now she surreptitiously gave morsels of it to Antony and Cleopatra, who were moving restlessly round the table, rubbing themselves against their legs and making it quite clear that it was their dinner-time.

The Duke took a second helping of rabbit.

There was a knock on the door.

"It will be Billy," Anthea said. "He has come to tell you about your horse."

The Duke put his hand in his pocket and drew out a handful of change.

"Can you afford six pence?" Anthea asked. "He has been very helpful to me."

"In which case why not a shilling?"

"We must not spoil the market!" she answered.

For a moment he saw a suspicion of her irresistible dimples.

She gave Billy the six pence, then remembered that the Duke had only had cider with his dinner.

"Is there anything you would like Billy to fetch you?" she asked. "I imagine The Pelican has some port."

"I would rather not risk it!" the Duke replied.

"That will be all, then, Billy."

"Good-night, Missie," he answered. "Oi'll be round early in th' morning with th' eggs for ye breakfast."

Anthea closed the door behind him.

The Duke had eaten practically all the rabbit and she put the few pieces which were left on a plate on the floor for Antony and Cleopatra.

He finished the strawberries in a few mouthfuls and helped himself to the cream-cheese which Anthea had made from the milk the cats had not required.

Anthea took the empty plates into the scullery. When she returned the Duke was cutting himself another piece of the loaf.

"I am afraid I cannot give you an adequate meal,"

she apologised in a worried voice, "but doubtless you can get something to eat at Pershore or wherever you are going to stay tonight."

The Duke finished the cheese before he replied:

"I think it would be sheer cruelty to take Hercules any further, and quite frankly I am tired."

"Why could you not have come here more slowly?" Anthea asked. "You know the doctor said you were to be careful not to do too much too quickly."

"I have a feeling," the Duke said with a note of amusement in his voice, "that is exactly the way your Nurse would have spoken to me were she here!"

"She would at least have made you behave sensibly!"

"If I am to be sensible," the Duke replied, "then I refuse categorically to go any further tonight!"

He looked round the tiny room before he added:

"I do not mind sleeping on the floor. I have slept in far worse places when we were fighting in Portugal."

"That is a ridiculous suggestion and you know it!" Anthea said sharply. "I can manage very well in the arm-chair, and I will show you where you can sleep."

She walked towards the very narrow, twisting staircase which was just beside the front door.

The Duke followed her.

"Be very careful of your head!" Anthea admonished. "Even I have difficulty coming up these stairs."

Doing as she had told him, the Duke followed her and she opened the door of the room above.

The walls sloped under the thatch but there were two low diamond-paned windows to let in the light and the Duke could see that the whole room was filled with a bed which made him stare in astonishment.

Anthea saw his face and for the first time since he had arrived she gave a little laugh.

"It is surprising, is it not?"

"It is indeed!" the Duke agreed.

"Nanny's brother-in-law weighed over twenty stone," Anthea explained, "and he always said he was so uncomfortable in an ordinary bed that he invented this one. He made the frame of oak and collected goose-feathers for his mattress."

Anthea's dimples were showing as she went on:

"When we were children Nanny used to tell us stories about this bed and how her sister, to make the sheets for it, had to sew two large ones together, and the same applied to the blankets.

"We used to talk about it as 'the Giant's Bed,' and when I saw it I knew it had been aptly named!"

"It certainly solves our problem," the Duke remarked.

"Yours, at any rate," Anthea answered. "I do not believe there is a bed at Axminster House as large as this one."

"There is not," the Duke agreed, "and that is why, as I have already said, it solves *our* problem."

Anthea looked at him enquiringly and he said:

"There is no reason for either you or me to sleep downstairs. If you take one side, and I the other, we might as well be in two different countries, France and England, for instance, with the Channel between us."

Anthea was silent and he said after a moment:

"It is a sensible solution and tomorrow, if you want me to, I will move on to Pershore, or any other place you suggest. But tonight I am going no further!"

He looked at Anthea challengingly, as if he expected her to argue. Then she said after a moment:

"Very . . . well. As you say, we have the Channel . . . between us . . . but I must point out that in the village they know me as 'Miss Forthingdale.' "

"Then we will certainly give them something to talk about!" the Duke said. "Unless of course you would like to put on your wedding-ring again."

Anthea was surprised he had noticed.

"The Vicar did not realise I was married and I thought it might be . . . uncomfortable to explain who I . . . was."

"I feel certain the Vicar will require an explanation after tonight!" the Duke said mockingly.

He turned towards the door.

"I am going to find Hercules because I have razors and various other necessities in my saddle-bag."

Anthea did not speak and he went on:

"When I come back I will want to wash and as I imagine the only place I can do so is downstairs, I suggest, Anthea, that you get into bed. If you are asleep when I come upstairs I will not wake you."

"Thank . . . you," Anthea said faintly.

She felt as if the Duke had taken command and there was nothing she could do but obey him.

He turned and left her, bending his head to get through the low door, and she heard him going rather cautiously down the twisting stairs.

She put her hands up to her cheeks as if to prevent them from burning.

She heard the door close and hurried down the stairs to take a kettle of hot water from the stove and stand it in the basin in the tiny scullery.

Then she returned to the bed-room and hastily began to undress.

It was growing late. Outside, dusk was falling, but there was still the last glow in the sky to throw a golden light through the open windows.

There was a fragrance of roses and stocks and Anthea could hear the rooks going to roost.

She did not light the candles, knowing that would bring in the moths. Instead, she left the curtains undrawn and, having put on one of the thin, lace-trimmed nightgowns which had been in her trousseau, she slipped into bed.

"I will pretend to be asleep," she told herself. "Then tomorrow I will make all the explanations that have to be made."

It seemed incredible that the Duke had eaten, they had talked, and yet they had not mentioned the reason why she had run away.

"He is tired," Anthea told herself, "and he probably feels he could not face a scene at the moment."

She was determined that there should not be one.

He might have endangered his health in travelling all that way to Yorkshire and she thought that once again it was her own thoughtlessness which was responsible.

"I should not have run away," she told herself accusingly.

She lay tense and trembling a little because there was so much for which she felt responsible.

And yet, even though she was nervous, it was impossible not to feel that the hard lump of unhappiness, which had lain in her breast ever since she left London, had vanished.

She was with the Duke again! He was there! She could listen to his voice and he was even more wonderful than she had remembered!

She did not dare ask herself why he had troubled to follow her.

Could it be that he was so angry that he wanted them to separate from each other forever?

She knew this was a thought that had lain at the back of her mind all the time and which frightened her more than anything else.

"Oh, please, God, let me see him . . . sometimes," she prayed. "Please, God . . . please . . ."

She heard his footsteps coming up the garden path. He shut the door and locked it, and she heard him crossing the room downstairs.

He was undressing, then she knew from the sound that he was washing in the small scullery at the back of the cottage.

She hoped he would find the soap and towel.

She should have put everything ready for him but she had been so bemused that she could think only of obeying his instructions and getting into bed as he had ordered her to do.

Now she could hear him coming up the stairs, and because she was shy, she shut her eyes as he opened the door of the bed-room and came in.

His side of the bed was only a few feet inside the door.

With her eyes shut, Anthea felt him get in and sink down in the feather mattress.

She held her breath, wondering if he would turn

over and go to sleep. But after a moment, as if he knew she was awake, he said conversationally:

"This is the most comfortable bed I have ever slept in."

"As you are so . . . tired, I am sure you . . . would sleep . . . anywhere."

"I am not as tired as I was," he said, "and I am no longer worried about you, Anthea."

"You were . . . worried?"

"Of course I was! How could you do anything so damnable as to run away without telling me where you were going? It was only after Dorkins announced dinner that I learnt you had gone!"

"I . . . I am . . . sorry," Anthea said in a very small voice.

"Why did you go?"

Anthea was so surprised at the question that she turned her head to look at him.

It was difficult to see clearly in the little light that remained in the room, but although his head was on the pillow he was looking towards her.

"Y-you . . . know why I . . . went," she managed to say after a moment.

"You thought I would be angry," the Duke said, "and I can understand that. But I wish you had trusted me."

"I . . . I wanted to tell you . . . when we were in . . . Brussels, but I was . . . afraid."

"Thais told me that you were trying to make some money because you were all so poor. I should have realised how very poor you were, Anthea."

There was a kindness in his voice which made Anthea feel suddenly very weak.

She had expected him to be angry, she had expected him to demand an explanation, but kindness was something she had not expected.

She stared at the window in front of her, feeling the tears come into her eyes.

"Thais told me that the hundred pounds you obtained for the cartoons enabled you all to have extra food which you had never enjoyed before. As always, Anthea, you were thinking of your family."

The tears ran down Anthea's cheeks but she did not wipe them away.

'If I do not move,' she thought to herself, 'he will not notice.'

There was silence before the Duke asked:

"Are you crying, Anthea?"

"N-no."

It was not a very convincing reply and after a moment he said:

"Are you sure you are not crying?"

It was impossible for Anthea to answer him.

"To make certain," the Duke said, "I am going to cross the Channel to see for myself. I do not want you to be unhappy."

Anthea gave a little sob and then her hands went up to her face.

"I . . . I am . . . sorry . . ." she began to say, then burst into tears.

She had not felt him move but he was beside her and his arms went round her as she cried:

"I am . . . s-sorry . . . I did not . . . mean it . . . I swear I did not m-mean it . . . I did not want to be . . . u-unkind to God-mama or really to . . . y-you . . . it just . . . h-happened and I am so . . . ashamed . . . so terribly a-ashamed at . . . what I have . . . done."

It was impossible to say any more.

She could only cry despairingly against him, all the misery of the last fortnight accumulating in a tempest which shook her whole body.

"It is all right," the Duke said gently. "It is all right."

She went on crying, realising she should stop herself but quite unable to do so.

There was something very comforting about feeling his arms holding her close. Then as her tears abated a little he said softly:

"It is all over. We can forget about it."

"We . . . cannot! We cannot do . . . that!" Anthea sobbed. "It was unlucky to . . . laugh at . . . love

. . . and because . . . I did so . . . you . . . had to . . . marry me."

"I have realised that," the Duke said quietly, "and that is why I have something to tell you."

Anthea stiffened.

She knew, she thought, what he was about to say.

"When I thought it over," he said, "I realised that it was very lucky for me that you did draw that particular cartoon."

Anthea thought she could not have heard him aright.

She raised her face, wet with her tears, to look up at him.

"It is quite simple, my darling. If you had not drawn it we would not have been married and we would not be here now."

As the Duke spoke he bent his head and his lips found hers.

For a moment Anthea was too astonished to breathe. Then as his mouth took possession of her she felt a strange streak like quicksilver flash through her.

It was so vivid, so poignant, that for a moment it was sheer pain, until it turned into an unbelievable rapture.

He drew her closer and his lips became more possessive, more insistent, and she felt her whole body invaded with a warmth and a wonder she had never known before.

It was an ecstasy which was beyond words, almost beyond thought, and it made her quiver with the glory of it.

'This is love!' she thought. 'This is what Mama said it was like and it is even more marvellous!'

Instinctively she drew closer to him, her body against his, her heart beating wildly, her lips very soft as she surrendered herself to the wonder of his lips.

The Duke raised his head.

"My darling one! My sweet!" he said unsteadily.

"I love . . . you!" Anthea whispered. "I love . . . you!"

Then the Duke was kissing her again, kissing her

passionately, demandingly, masterfully, until she could
no longer think.

She only knew that her love reached out to him
so that she gave him not only her lips, but her heart,
her soul, and her . . . body.

They were one and there was nothing else but
love.

* * *

The moon shone through the small window,
throwing a silver light onto the bed.

"Are you . . . asleep?" Anthea whispered.

"I am too happy to sleep," the Duke answered.

"But you must try. You have ridden such a long
way today."

"Are you still molly-coddling me?" he asked with
a note of amusement in his voice, and pulled her nearer to him. "Oh, my precious little love, I cannot tell
you how much I missed you when you were not there
to bully me, to make me take care of myself!"

"I thought . . . you would be . . . glad to be . . . rid
of me."

"I think what I missed most," the Duke said, "was
your laughter. I have never known that days could
be so long, so dull and lifeless!"

"I laughed . . . at love. . . ."

"Which you will never do again, my adorable
wife! We will laugh together, but like the gods, only
from sheer happiness."

"Together."

Anthea's cheek was against his shoulder.

"I suppose I fell in love with your dimples," he
ruminated. "They fascinate me. And your voice has
some lilting quality in it that I have never heard in
any other woman's."

Anthea gave a deep sigh.

"I was . . . always thinking how much I must . . .
bore you after the brilliant and beautiful women you
have known and . . . loved."

Her voice trembled on the last word.

"I know now," the Duke answered, "that I have
never really been in love before. I have been attracted,

enamoured, passionately aroused by many women, but I have never laughed with them."

"But you wanted to . . . make love . . . to them," Anthea murmured.

"I wanted to make love to you, too, but you would not let me."

"I have often . . . thought during these . . . last weeks how . . . foolish it was of me."

"No, you were right!" the Duke said. "I was not offering you real love, Anthea, not at that moment! But when we were in Brussels I found it increasingly hard not to touch you, and not to come to your room after we had gone to bed."

"Why did you . . not do . . . so?"

"I suppose the truth was that I was too proud to risk being rebuffed for the second time," he answered, "but every day I wanted you more. Every night was a frustration I hope never to repeat, knowing you were so near, and yet the doors between us were closed."

"Is that . . . why you suggested we . . . sleep here . . . tonight?" Anthea asked.

"I will admit that fate played into my hands by producing a bed like this," the Duke answered, "but I had no intention, Anthea, of letting you escape me a second time!"

She gave a little cry.

"I am glad . . . so very glad!"

"Thais was sure you loved me, even if you were not aware of it."

"Thais?" Anthea questioned. "But how could she have known?"

"Perhaps you are so close as a family that the girls know more about you than you know yourself. That is something I missed by being an only child."

"Thais was right!" Anthea said. "I love you more than I can ever tell you! I love you with . . . every breath I draw . . . with every thought . . . I think. There is only . . . you!"

The Duke kissed her forehead, her eyes, her mouth, and then her neck where a little pulse was beating madly.

"I had no idea any woman could be so sweet, so soft, so adorable!" he said.

There was a note of passion in his voice that made Anthea quiver.

"I will . . . try to be exactly as you . . . want me to be, and I promise I will . . . never draw a picture again!"

"I have every intention that you shall draw."

"You . . . want me to?" Anthea asked incredulously.

"Not cartoons, my precious, except to amuse me," he said. "But you obviously have an extraordinary talent which I do not think should be wasted!"

Anthea waited, wide-eyed.

"What I suggested—and I have been planning this all the time I have been trying to find you—is that you should have lessons from an artist who is really qualified to teach."

"Perhaps I can only . . . caricature people?"

"We will find out for certain," the Duke replied, "and I suggest we start by going to Italy."

"To Italy?" Anthea exclaimed.

"I have, my sweet darling, been defrauded of a proper honeymoon!"

He kissed her small nose before he said:

"I have always understood that a honeymoon is a time for love-making."

He paused before he asked:

"That is, if you agree, my sweetheart."

Anthea felt a little flame within her vibrate to the note in his voice.

"I . . . agree," she murmured against him.

He kissed her hair.

"I want to teach you about love, my darling, and I promise you that you will never escape me again."

"I . . . will . . . not want . . . to do so. . . ."

He kissed both her dimples before he continued:

"I do not think either of us wishes to go back to London at the moment. So I suggest we cross the real

Channel again and travel to Italy, the Paradise of artists."

"I would love that!" Anthea cried. "I would love anywhere with you . . . but especially Italy!"

"You shall study the works of Michelangelo in Florence," the Duke said, "and perhaps we will find someone to give you some lessons there before we visit Venice, and then come home via Paris. There are some drawings in the Louvre I particularly want you too see."

"It sounds too . . . thrilling . . . too perfect!"

"And when we get back," the Duke went on, "I think there are many things at Axminster House in Hampshire that will please you. But I know now it has always lacked something which you and I must provide."

"What is that?" Anthea enquired.

He held her very close to him and his lips moved over the softness of her skin before he answered:

"A family, my adorable wife. It is what I missed when I had no Thais, Chloe, or Phebe with whom to laugh."

His lips were touching hers as he asked:

"Will you give me beautiful daughters like you, my lovely one?"

He felt the quiver which ran through her before she whispered:

"Only if . . . you will . . . give me lots of . . . sons exactly like you . . ."

She was unable to finish the sentence because he was kissing her with a passion that revealed the fire within him.

It evoked an answering flame in Anthea and she clung to him, knowing that once again he had aroused the incredible rapture and the blinding glory that she had always known was a part of real love.

It was everything which was beautiful and sacred, everything that she had heard in music, seen in painting, and found in poetry.

It was divine and she must surrender herself to it completely and wholeheartedly.

The Duke's lips became more insistent.

She could feel his hand touching her body, could feel his heart beating against hers.

Then there was only love and the laughter of the gods.

ABOUT THE AUTHOR

BARBARA CARTLAND, the celebrated romantic author, historian, playwright, lecturer, political speaker and television personality, has now written over 150 books. Miss Cartland has had a number of historical books published and several biographical ones, including that of her brother, Major Ronald Cartland, who was the first Member of Parliament to be killed in the War. This book had a Foreword by Sir Winston Churchill.

In private life, Barbara Cartland, who is a Dame of the Order of St. John of Jerusalem, has fought for better conditions and salaries for Midwives and nurses. As president of the Royal College of Midwives (Hertfordshire Branch), she has been invested with the first Badge of Office ever given in Great Britain, which was subscribed to by the Midwives themselves. She has also championed the cause for old people and founded the first Romany Gypsy Camp in the world.

Barbara Cartland is deeply interested in Vitamin Therapy and is President of the British National Association for Health.

Barbara Cartland

The world's bestselling author of romantic fiction. Her stories are always captivating tales of intrigue, adventure and love.

☐	THE TEARS OF LOVE	2148	$1.25
☐	THE DEVIL IN LOVE	2149	$1.25
☐	THE ELUSIVE EARL	2436	$1.25
☐	THE BORED BRIDEGROOM	6381	$1.25
☐	JOURNEY TO PARADISE	6383	$1.25
☐	THE PENNILESS PEER	6387	$1.25
☐	NO DARKNESS FOR LOVE	6427	$1.25
☐	THE LITTLE ADVENTURE	6428	$1.25
☐	LESSONS IN LOVE	6431	$1.25
☐	THE DARING DECEPTION	6435	$1.25
☐	CASTLE OF FEAR	8103	$1.25
☐	THE GLITTERING LIGHTS	8104	$1.25
☐	A SWORD TO THE HEART	8105	$1.25
☐	THE MAGNIFICENT MARRIAGE	8166	$1.25
☐	THE RUTHLESS RAKE	8240	$1.25
☐	THE DANGEROUS DANDY	8280	$1.25
☐	THE WICKED MARQUIS	8467	$1.25
☐	LOVE IS INNOCENT	8505	$1.25
☐	THE FRIGHTENED BRIDE	8780	$1.25
☐	THE FLAME IS LOVE	8887	$1.25

Buy them at your local bookseller or use this handy coupon:

Barbara Cartland

The world's bestselling author of romantic fiction. Her stories are always captivating tales of intrigue, adventure and love.

☐	A VERY NAUGHTY ANGEL	2107	$1.25
☐	THE CRUEL COUNT	2128	$1.25
☐	CALL OF THE HEART	2140	$1.25
☐	AS EAGLES FLY	2147	$1.25
☐	THE MASK OF LOVE	2366	$1.25
☐	AN ARROW OF LOVE	2426	$1.25
☐	A GAMBLE WITH HEARTS	2430	$1.25
☐	A KISS FOR THE KING	2433	$1.25
☐	A FRAME OF DREAMS	2434	$1.25
☐	THE FRAGRANT FLOWER	2435	$1.25
☐	MOON OVER EDEN	2437	$1.25
☐	THE GOLDEN ILLUSION	2449	$1.25
☐	FIRE ON THE SNOW	2450	$1.25
☐	THE HUSBAND HUNTERS	2461	$1.25
☐	THE SHADOW OF SIN	6430	$1.25
☐	SAY YES, SAMANTHA	7834	$1.25
☐	THE KARMA OF LOVE	8106	$1.25
☐	BEWITCHED	8630	$1.25
☐	THE IMPETUOUS DUCHESS	8705	$1.25

Bantam Book Catalog

It lists over a thousand money-saving best-sellers originally priced from $3.75 to $15.00 —bestsellers that are yours now for as little as 60¢ to $2.95!

The catalog gives you a great opportunity to build your own private library at huge savings!

So don't delay any longer—send us your name and address and 25¢ (to help defray postage and handling costs).